DO NOT RESUSCITATE

DO NOT RESUSCITATE

or

The Monkey Parade

Nicholas Ponticello

BOOLEANOP, WOODLAND, CA

To Nico—for bringing me to life

FOREWORD

ANCIENT ALCHEMISTS, despite having accomplished nothing for which history has any reason to remember them, became legendary for their tireless quest to conceive a magic formula that would take an ordinary substance, like iron or lead, and transmogrify it into yet another ordinary substance, gold, which humans have, incidentally, singled out to be of more value than all the other ordinary substances in the universe.

It was a futile endeavor, however, for it turns out ordinary substances such as lead and iron are composed of tiny little particles—namely protons, electrons, bosons, and so on— invisible to the naked eye, but which are so tightly linked arm in arm that the process of taking them apart and putting them back together again in any coherent manner takes a great deal of energy, which, as it turns out, takes a great deal of gold. A conundrum.

Incidentally, scientists today are trying to do the same thing as these ancient wizards, but instead of making gold out of lead, they are trying to make something potable, like freshwater, out of something toxic, like the ocean.

Here, again, a lot of energy and gold must be applied with great persistence for anything to get done.

The lesson: some things, once altered, are not easily undone.

Ancient alchemists, moreover, concerned themselves with an even higher aim. They sought to develop an elixir capable of granting the drinker the gift of immortal life. One might argue pharmaceutical companies are the distant cousins of these prehistoric potion masters.

They called the alchemists' quest for immortality the Magnum Opus, the Great Work.

In the following true account, the author refers with regular occasion to the Magnum Opus. While the staging of these references is sometimes confounding and tends to interrupt the flow of the narrative, it was in the better judgment of this editor to let the text alone, for who can say what profound implications may be lurking in the flotsam and jetsam of a dying man's last words?   —NP

CHAPTER 1

MY NAME IS JIM LORENZO FROST, and at the end of April, I will download my brain to a microchip no bigger than a thumbnail. The microchip will be stored in a titanium canister in a warehouse at Humanity Co. until the specialists there figure out a tidy way to get my brain off the microchip and back into a human body, preferably my own, or at least a copy of my own.

It isn't my idea of a good time. My daughter Eliza talked me into it. She says it is common practice now to back up your brain. She has hers done every year or so, like a teeth cleaning or a routine trip to the doctor. She says almost everybody does it nowadays. I don't know what everybody thinks they've got up there that's so important.

Nevertheless, I agreed to it. Not because it makes any

sense to me. I still remember the phone number of my best friend in elementary school, little Frankie Mahoney: 310-746-2275. Undoubtedly the number has changed, or Frankie is dead. So who needs a microchip for that kind of thing? Useless information.

Nevertheless, if downloading my brain onto a microchip will help Eliza sleep at night, well then that's that. My dear Eliza needs all the sleep she can get. She has what they used to call a nervous condition. Today they call it generalized anxiety disorder. I think that's the same thing my mother had. She just called it the jitters.

The motive for backing up your brain is simple: to live forever. At the present moment, the said objective is impossible. They can get everything out of your head, or so they say, and package it nicely in a shiny titanium canister that you can put on your mantel, or in a trophy case, or bury in your attic. But they don't have the foggiest idea how to get all that hogwash back into your head if, say, you suffer from memory loss or Alzheimer's disease, or you die and you want to upload your memories to a clone. For now everybody's memories just sit in a warehouse somewhere gathering dust. And that's what Eliza would like for me, too: my very own dust-gathering microchip. As if the graves of the dead don't gather enough dust already.

Eliza has three girls of her own. The eldest has just graduated college: Stanford. I was a Berkeley man myself, but I managed to get through my granddaughter's commencement without hissing. That's what we Berkeley Bears do when we come across a Stanford Cardinal: We hiss. And sometimes we make a chopping motion at our necks. But I try to keep such impulses to myself.

Eliza's eldest girl is named Marilee after my deceased sister, may she rest in peace. And goodness knows my sister Marilee is resting in peace somewhere, or resting nowhere at all if that's how it goes after you die. But at least she's not buzzing around on a microchip waiting to be brought back from the dead. The technology for that kind of thing wasn't around when she died. So I think it is safe to say my sister Marilee is gone for good. Done. Finished. Kaput.

Which brings me to my point. I cannot say I want to be gone for good. And although I am not wild about putting all my memories onto a microchip, I can't say I'm opposed to putting a few of my memories onto paper so that little Marilee Junior or whoever else happens along might hear from me from time to time and know that I was once futzing around on this planet.

Seventy-three years I have been futzing around on this planet. And that's how I suppose most people begin their biographies: I was born seventy-three years ago, on February 26, 1983, to Jonas Frost, the owner of an antique shop, and Anita Lorenzo, his pretty Italian wife.

CHAPTER 2

"IS IT GOING TO KILL ME?" I asked when Eliza told me I was going to have my brain downloaded to a microchip.

It's a question I ask a lot these days. "Is it going to kill me?" When I climb a long flight of stairs or get behind the wheel of a car or choke on a half-chewed bit of steak. Is having my brain downloaded onto a microchip going to kill me?

Eliza assures me it will not. But I can't help wondering. If my thoughts, my memories, my preferences, my impulses—all the things that make me *me*—are going to be transferred onto a single, tiny microchip, then where does that leave *me*, the original me?

"It's just a *copy*," Eliza says.

But if I can manage to be in two places at once—well I don't know what that means for the existence of a soul.

My dear Eliza has had her brain downloaded sixteen times, and she certainly doesn't seem any less herself than before. Far from it. Today she called me on the phone to fuss over my hair. It's always too long or too short or too gray. Eliza fusses over a lot of things. When she was in preschool, Eliza couldn't put her socks on without making sure the seam lined up perfectly with her toes. And try to get her to drink a glass of milk a day past the expiration date—forget about it! You might as well ask a chimpanzee to recite the Gettysburg Address. That's Eliza.

My other daughter, Eliza's sister, however, turned out to be quite the opposite. Kendra Ann. A lovely sensible girl. She is married to a British Indian who works as a venture capitalist in London. They have two boys, an oddity in a family prone to spawning girls.

Their mother, my wife, is now dead. Cancer. She is also gone for good. I think that is why Eliza is so keen on getting my brain downloaded. Eliza lost her mother when she was ten, and she has been worried every day since that I'm just as likely to blink out of existence. Maybe I am. We all are, I guess. But Eliza assures me this microchip will soon solve that problem.

CHAPTER 3

I HAVE MY ORDERS FROM ELIZA: haircut, Fort Mason Center, two o'clock. After all, tonight is the banquet for the retired men and women of the SHEM Project, and I am the guest of honor.

The organizers have asked me to give a speech. I haven't prepared anything yet. I was thinking of winging it. Eliza won't hear of it, though. She said, "Dad, you can't *wing it*! That's how people end up on YouTube!"

"Don't tell me how people end up on YouTube," I barked at Eliza. "When I was little Marilee's age, I was a YouTube sensation!"

It's true. I was.

But Eliza will never know if I decide to wing it or not because she isn't going to the banquet tonight. It is a well-known fact in the Frost family that Eliza is afraid of crowds. She is sending her three girls in her stead: Marilee Junior, Luanne, and Joyce.

Eliza's husband is not going to be there either. He is overseas negotiating a water trade in Sudan.

Good luck!

I started working for the SHEM Project when I was twenty-three. I was just out of college and didn't know what I wanted to do with my life when I saw an advertisement on Craigslist for a courier service in the East Bay. I sent an application to the contact listed and received an e-mail from Happy Happy Happy Message Runners, Inc. The e-mail was only three sentences:

> Thank you for applying to Happy Happy Happy Message Runners, Inc. Payments will be made upon receipt of goods. Within the next few weeks, you will receive an e-mail containing the details of your first assignment.

I thought it was a joke. And I didn't hear another word from them for nearly two weeks, so I got a job at the Berkeley Art Museum standing around the gallery, telling guests to shut up and to keep their hands to themselves. I had been at it only a few days, and I had become quite the expert at giving fussy, screaming kids the evil eye, when I received my next e-mail from Happy Happy Happy Message Runners, Inc. It read:

Dear Mr. Frost,

Please retrieve luggage for passenger "Adrian Jacobs" from United flight 467, arriving at the Oakland International Airport on June 13 at 4:37 p.m. Deliver directly to Genova Delicatessen on Fifty-First and Telegraph. Look for the man in the yellow jacket.

Thank you for your service.
Happy Happy Happy Message Runners, Inc.

I was scheduled to work at the museum on June 13, the day of the delivery. So I called a friend of mine, Charlie McAllister, who had gotten me the job at the Berkeley Art Museum, and I asked him if he could cover for me. Since Charlie had a habit of blowing his paycheck on pot, he took the shift no questions asked.

I had to look up the metro lines that would get me to the airport and then to Fifty-First and Telegraph since I didn't have a car at the time, and my sole mode of transportation around the Bay in those days was the neon-green eighteen-speed road bike I had inherited from a crazy roommate that moved to Hawaii one summer and never came back for his stuff. Last I heard he had joined the Navy SEALs.

The museum paid about eleven dollars an hour. And after taxes I usually walked away with something like $300 a week, which was good money for a broke graduate in a garbage economy. Although they were calling it a recession, it wasn't quite so bad then as it is now. With the price of everything today what it is, $300 a week might pay the water bill for a month. But back then it was decent money.

As I hopped on BART toward the Coliseum, where I would catch a shuttle to the airport, I considered whether delivering one stinking package could possibly make up for the lousy sixty bucks I was supposed to make that day at the museum. I was real hard up for cash in those days, and I didn't want to take out another loan from my parents, who were always so uptight about money and seemed to resent their children for never returning big on their "investment," which is what they had called us as far back as I can remember.

I had to ask myself if this little excursion was worth it. The fare for the BART ride alone would cost me my dinner.

But the e-mail from Happy Happy Happy Message Runners, Inc. had been so deliberately surreptitious that I figured, what the hell?

When I arrived at the Coliseum stop, I got turned around at the station and ended up missing my shuttle, which put me about ten minutes behind schedule. I started to get nervous that I'd be late and that some bum would snatch up the luggage before I arrived.

I didn't even know what the luggage was supposed to look like. All I had was a flight number and a passenger name: Adrian Jacobs.

The airport was a mess. Back then you could book a flight from Oakland to Los Angeles for forty-nine bucks. So people were flying in and out of the Bay Area all of the time. When gas prices skyrocketed in the twenties, the era of affordable air travel came to an end.

I checked the arrivals kiosk for flight 467. The plane had arrived on time from Chicago, and passengers were directed to baggage carousel A2. When I got there, the carousel had already been picked clean, and all that was left on the conveyor belt were three large suitcases, what looked like a laptop bag, and a small red ice cooler, the kind paramedics use to convey donor organs.

I felt a little shifty approaching the carousel. The TSA

officers didn't take much notice of me, not until I started thumbing the ID tags on all the bags. The last tag I checked belonged to the red cooler, and lo and behold, it read, "Adrian Jacobs."

A TSA officer who had been watching me paw through the bags started toward me to offer assistance or to whisk me off to airport jail—I didn't stick around long enough to find out. I swept up the red cooler in a hurry and made a beeline for the door.

The cooler was light, no more than a few pounds. And I tried to imagine what it could contain that required hand delivery in lieu of UPS or FedEx shipping. Clearly something with an expiration date, I thought, seeing the beads of condensation form on the cooler's white lid.

This is the point in the story where people usually ask me if I looked inside the cooler. And I say that I battled the urge all the way to Genova Delicatessen. I like to say, "It was a question of ethics," or some other such thing, "and in the end, I had the willpower not to look."

Which isn't exactly true. Granted, I never looked inside the cooler, but the reason I never looked doesn't have anything to do with ethics, per se. I just didn't want to know what it contained, not *really*.

It could have been a bomb or crack cocaine or a kidney, and I didn't dare mix myself up in a mess like that. As far as I was concerned, so long as I didn't know what I was carrying, I was an innocent man.

How's that for ethics?

I was young, and it's hard to imagine getting caught up in anything really serious when you are only twenty-three. Life just *isn't* serious when you're twenty-three. At least it wasn't for me back in the year 2006. I suppose it's a bit more serious for twenty-three-year-olds now, what with the water shortages and the collapse of the economy and everything.

But back then I had the philosophy that ignorance equated to innocence, or some other such nonsense. And, therefore, it didn't matter if it was twenty kilos of crack cocaine in the red cooler, or a bull elephant's tusks, so long as I never found out about it.

I took BART and then a bus to Fifty-First and Telegraph. When I walked into Genova Delicatessen, I had the feeling that everybody was staring at me, staring at the red cooler.

It's more likely that nobody was staring at me because nobody in the whole place could have known what the hell was going on. I certainly didn't. But I felt like the red ice cooler stood out like a sore thumb, and I couldn't wait to ditch the thing. I looked around for a man in a yellow jacket, and not finding any trace of him, I started to get nervous. I decided to order a sandwich so as not to look too conspicuous. Meanwhile the red cooler sat across from me at the little table, wanting to explode its mysterious contents all over the room.

After about half an hour, a police officer came into the deli, and I just about pissed myself. In the time it took me to finish my sandwich, I became convinced that I had gotten mixed up in an international organ-trafficking scheme and that the red cooler contained the liver of a kidnapped child from Guatemala, or some other such horror.

My palms were sweating and my pulse was racing as the cop put in an order for a sandwich and then paced about the room waiting for his number to be called.

I was trying my best not to call attention to myself, and I was kicking myself for finishing my sandwich in such a hurry because now I had nothing left to do except sit there and pretend to be caught up in a text conversation on my phone.

And just when I thought my nerves couldn't handle the suspense, a man stepped into the delicatessen wearing blue jeans and a bright-yellow jacket. He looked around the shop, his eyes lingered momentarily on the red cooler, and then he stepped up to the counter and ordered two sandwiches.

I watched his movements intently, wondering how I should make myself known without alerting the suspicion of the cop.

But then the cop's number was called, and he picked up his sandwich and left, at which point the man in the yellow jacket walked straight over to me and sat down.

"I ordered you a sandwich. But it looks like you already ate," he said, indicating the residual crumbs and wax paper on the table.

"Sorry about that," I said.

"No worries. Is that it?" he asked, pointing to the cooler.

"Yeah," I said.

The man in the yellow jacket pulled out a thick envelope and slid it across the table, just like I had seen done in gangster movies. I was too terrified to pick it up, so I just left it there burning a hole in the laminate tabletop.

"They just called my number," the man said, and he got up to retrieve the sandwiches. When he came back, he didn't sit down. He tossed a sandwich down in front of me, grabbed the cooler, and walked out the door without another word.

When I got home, I finally opened the envelope. It contained $200 cash.

Maybe at tonight's banquet, in lieu of a speech, I can tell

the story of the man in the yellow jacket and the red cooler and the $200 cash. I bet they'll get a kick out of it.

Except everyone at the banquet is already going to know exactly what was in that red cooler.

CHAPTER 4

YOU'LL NEVER GUESS what happened to me last night. I was standing over a plate of stuffed artichokes, thinking what a great speech I had just made, when a man walked up to me. He looked about a hundred years old, and his eyes were cloudy with cataracts. He was grinning from ear to ear.

"How'd you like the sandwich?" he asked.

It was the man in the yellow coat! He was wearing forest-green slacks and a camel hair jacket, and he had aged so dramatically that I didn't recognize him at first. I had always imagined he had wound up dead in an alley somewhere, killed over the contents of the red cooler. As it turns out, he's a biology teacher now.

He introduced himself as George Ainsley, and he told me he's the oldest teacher in the San Francisco Unified School

District. All these years we've been shopping at the same Whole Foods!

We agreed to have lunch sometime, *at our old spot*, he joked. I think he has a wonderful sense of humor for an old fart. I myself am surprised at how quickly a sense of humor can atrophy with age. I can't think of anything more important to keep in tip-top shape than a sense of humor, especially after your knees and hair and sight and taste and smell and even little parts of your mind are gone. Even after most of the people you knew or ever could have known have died. Even after you can no longer pee in a straight line anymore, and instead you splatter the bathroom with urine in the pattern of a poorly aimed shotgun. It would all be so goddamned depressing if it weren't so goddamned funny.

It was a trip reliving the old days with George Ainsley. George and I never crossed paths again after that day at Genova Delicatessen, but we have a lot of shared memories about SHEM, and it turns out George knew Greta, my now-deceased wife.

I told my daughter Eliza all this last night on the phone when I got home. She makes me call her every morning when I wake up and every night before I go to bed—to make certain I'm not dead. I told her that George Ainsley was about the funniest old-timer I had met in quite some time.

"Do you really think it's a good idea to go on making friends at your age?" Eliza scolded. "It just means one more funeral to attend."

The dry, mildly sarcastic sense of humor on which I reared my children manifested as cynicism in Eliza. Eliza got all the cynicism, I think. And Kendra Ann and Spencer got all the humor.

My son, Spencer, called me, too, to see how the speech went. He would have been there if it weren't for the distance. He lives in New York City. His husband was in a biking accident Saturday along the Hudson River, and he needed to stay home to take care of things. Eugene is drinking through a straw, Spencer tells me. But he'll be okay. They have two adopted children, girls.

We're a family of girls. I had five sisters. I have two daughters. And now I have five granddaughters. Before Kendra Ann's two little boys came along, Spencer and I were the only men in the family, which is, I think, why we are so close.

I had a thought. This would be a good place to draw some sort of family tree since there are so many names to remember. So here it goes:

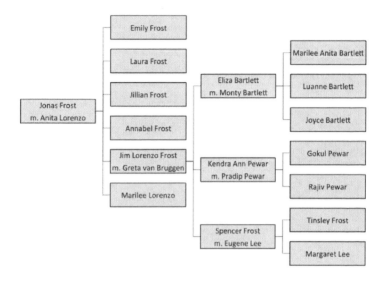

There are no less than thirteen woman in our family tree if you count my mother, and only five men if you count my father. And now looking at the family tree, I realize the Frost family name is about as good as dead.

Good-bye, Frosts, forever!

I am Jim Lorenzo Frost, if that was not already clear. And my father was Jonas Frost. He was originally from Minnesota, but he moved to Los Angeles in 1972 with his best friend, Rick Milliken, to get into the automobile trade.

He and Rick collected old cars, restored them, and sold them at a profit to car collectors who then, in turn, sold them to other car collectors and so on.

Their business started in Minnesota. They had about fifteen cars holed up in a warehouse somewhere. In the summer of 1972, they drove all the way out to California in search of the best old car parts.

Why does Los Angeles have all the best old car parts?

No rust.

In 1972 Los Angeles wasn't the dump it is now. Back then nobody was worried about all the water running out, and about the average temperatures rising four degrees, and about all the climate refugees. Back then people worried about getting a tee time or finding a nice pattern of wallpaper or choosing a bottle of wine. First World problems, my buddy Charlie used to call them.

And those were the kinds of problems my father had when he moved into a Motel 6 up in Sunland. He was worried about how he was going to find the best deals on car parts, beat the other guys to them, and then get the other guys to pay more for them. That was the nature of my father's First World problems in 1972.

In those days they didn't have cell phones or the Internet or a data cloud. They had a newspaper and a pay phone.

Every day Rick and my father received a 4:00 a.m. wake-up call from the front desk. They were on the road by 5:00 a.m. and at the *Sun Valley Tribune* by 6:00 a.m., where they'd get the first copy of the classifieds hot off the press.

Then they'd hurry over to the pay phone on the corner of Foothill and Oro Vista and phone up each listing for a dime apiece. And they'd butter up these folks who didn't have the faintest idea what their cars were worth, and who couldn't be more grateful to my dear old dad for taking them off their hands.

And right there on the phone, in just five minutes' time, my dad would make them feel as if they'd known him for years. It was my dad's way of marking his territory. Pissing on a fire hydrant, so to speak. If anybody else came along to buy the parts before my dad could get to them, the owner would say, "Oh, I got a call this morning from a buddy of mine out in Sunland, so they're no longer for sale," even if a better offer came along.

Nobody could refuse my dad. He had a voice like salted caramel, which he used to woo buyers, sellers, and feminine types. And he was handsome to boot. So people naturally trusted him. Handsome people never have to work very hard for trust.

After my dad and Rick ran through the classifieds, they had to map out where they wanted to go and how they wanted to get there. This they did on real maps made of compressed fiber from trees! None of this "Destination will be on your left" mumbo jumbo.

They brought the cars back to the Motel 6 in Sunland and parked them all over the lot. The spare parts, which were really what the business was all about, filled the drawers and tables and even the tub of the motel room. They paid off the cleaning staff to deliver clean sheets every week and to otherwise stay out of the way. And they lived like this, in the Motel 6, for eighteen months, buying and selling and buying and selling.

Whatever they purchased, they'd mark up 30, 50, 100 percent and pocket the profit. They were shipping all over Los Angeles County under the pseudonym Franklin Brothers Used Cars & Parts.

And boy were they ever making money. You wouldn't know it, the way they were living day to day out of a motel, eating nothing but McDonald's apple pies and Wendy's burgers. But after about eighteen months, they must have had twenty cars out in the parking lot at any given time, and at least two shipments of parts going out every day. They were living out a phenomenon that used to be more common back then. It was called the American Dream.

Then one day my dad came back from another day living the dream and found a note from the motel manager taped to the door of their room. The motel manager, a middle-aged divorcee by the name of Harvey Lemming, wanted to see my dear old dad right away. He wanted to know exactly how many cars my dad had parked out in the motel lot.

In the manager's office, there was a little electric fan whirring away on his desk, and behind him the thermostat was set to eighty-two degrees, and heat was being pumped in through a vent in the ceiling.

"That's a sign of a man who doesn't know what he wants," my dad used to say telling the story at cocktail parties and weddings. "Doesn't even know if he's hot or cold. That's the kind of a fella desperate to be *told* what he wants."

So my dad told Harvey Lemming just how many cars were parked out in the motel lot. And then he told Harvey Lemming that he was just the kind of man who deserved to own one.

Harvey Lemming told my dad he couldn't keep all those cars there anymore. And he told my dad to be out in a week. And then Harvey Lemming bought a 1962 Corvette convertible.

Rick moved back to Minnesota after that. My dad stayed in California and bought the antique shop. That was how it all went.

I was born after all of this, of course. My dad didn't even

meet my mom until 1975. And I had no idea until later that my father was a hustler. To me and my friends, he was just a washed-up car salesman with an affection for old things. It wasn't until many years later that I learned my dad didn't have a nostalgic bone in his body.

The day my mom and sisters drove me up to Berkeley, my dad stayed behind to rent out my room.

CHAPTER 5

MY SON has just offered to take me to Paris for the summer, along with his husband and kids. He has been invited to teach a summer course on kinetic power and engineering at the École Polytechnique. He is fluent in French, of course, because of his mother. She spoke it perfectly and spoke it often, even though I couldn't understand a lick of it.

Spencer is invited all over the world to speak about kinetic power and engineering. In graduate school he invented an insert that can be installed in the bottom of a shoe to absorb all the kinetic energy wasted throughout the day walking around. The energy is then funneled into the main grid or into a generator to help power streets and homes. It's a nifty idea, if you ask me. Now people all over the world hold walkathons to generate energy.

Meanwhile, Spencer generates cash.

His husband, Eugene, is a writer and can go just about anywhere anytime he wants. Paris in the summer? Why not?

The kids are in the second and third grades. They have heaps of time in the summer, too. And they speak French perfectly. And English. And Mandarin because of Eugene.

They have asked me to join them on this eight-week sojourn because I am retired, and I, too, have heaps of time, not just in the summer, but all year round. I do not speak French or any other foreign language, but I do speak second and third grader, and that is an invaluable skill in any babysitter.

Incidentally, Greta and I were married in Paris.

Greta was born Greta Van Bruggen in Antwerp, Belgium. Van Bruggen is a Dutch name. Her ancestors were from Holland. However, the Van Bruggen family left Holland centuries ago. Her only living relative is her brother, Duncan Van Bruggen, who continues to live near Antwerp. I've only met him once, and that was after Greta died. She wished to have her ashes scattered over the small farm where she was brought up, the small farm that her brother inherited from their mother.

I wrote Duncan Van Bruggen after Greta died. He knew that she was ill, of course—Greta and Duncan wrote each other almost every day. I told Duncan that Greta had passed away on October 5 (the year was 2025; Greta was thirty-seven). I wanted to visit Antwerp in December to scatter her ashes on the farm.

His reply was brief. He said that it would mean a lot to him if I came. We would meet at last, the two men who loved her most in this life, and we would carry out her final wish together.

So I caught a flight to Belgium two days before Christmas. I left our motherless children in the care of my pal Charlie, who was living in the Mission District then, just a few blocks from where I live now.

I had to check the urn with Greta's ashes at the airport. They had a form for that sort of thing, which I filled out at check-in. I had brought along the death certificate and a notice from the crematorium, and a copy of Greta's last will and testament. I even brought along Greta's passport for good measure.

And then, somewhere between San Francisco and Brussels, the airline lost the urn. At the baggage claim in Brussels, a frazzled airline attendant approached me hesitantly to explain that my late wife had been misplaced.

I have never been much of a subscriber to the theory of

an afterlife. I have always believed when you're dead, you're dead. Gone. Kaput. However, when my dear Greta became a piece of lost luggage, I had the fleeting notion that somewhere up there, my dear old wife was pulling my leg.

You see, it was a case of lost airline luggage that led to my meeting Greta Van Bruggen in the first place.

It was *her* luggage that went missing so, so, so many years ago. And Happy Happy Happy Message Runners, Inc. hired *me* to find out where it had gone.

CHAPTER 6

HAPPY HAPPY HAPPY MESSAGE RUNNERS, INC. had me working upward of three jobs a week back then. Always a red cooler from a luggage carousel at the airport, either Oakland or San Francisco or all the way out in San Jose. I got around any way I could, riding the buses and trains, sometimes hopping on my bike or borrowing Charlie's car.

The drop-off was usually a local deli or a park. One time it was at the back of a bus. And every time there was somebody there in a brightly colored hat or scarf or sweater to meet me. I never saw the man in the yellow coat again, not until recently anyway. Every time it was someone new, and little more than a few words were exchanged before I traded the cooler for an envelope of cash.

I never bothered to look inside the coolers to see what it was I was getting paid in unmarked bills to smuggle from God knows where to God knows where. I was too scared. And I figured I could handle *not* knowing better than I could handle knowing.

I was just a kid, and I wasn't responsible for things I knew nothing about.

The first couple jobs paid $200 apiece, and then $300, and then $400. I quit my job at the museum and started seeing a girl I had known in college, Kate Drummond, who was really interested in cars, like my father, and who knew how to get the best pot in the Bay for a decent price. And that was how I wasted away the better part of a year.

I went home to Los Angeles for Christmas. My dad gave me a 2007 BMW 3 Series sedan that I drove back up to the Bay. I moved out of my apartment in Berkeley and into a studio in San Francisco to be closer to my sister Marilee, who had just graduated from the University of Chicago and had moved to the city for a job in corporate at Wells Fargo.

My other sisters were still living in Los Angeles.

At year-end I didn't report my earnings since I had always been paid in cash, and as far as I knew, I had not signed a contract with anybody anywhere, so I was as good as unemployed. Nevertheless I had made about $32,000 in six months on deliveries alone. All my work orders still came in the form of e-mails from Happy Happy Happy Message Runners, Inc.

I tried not to question the integrity of any of it.

It turned out my sister Marilee wasn't quite cut out for corporate, so after a year, she quit her job at Wells Fargo and enrolled in the San Francisco Art Institute using the money she had made in banking, which, she confided to me later, had been her plan all along.

My father was outraged. He said that a person cannot hope to survive in this world unless they are in the business of exploiting fools. He said art was the Novocain of fools. He asked Marilee if she wanted to be numb and dumb her whole life. That was an expression my father used to use a lot on us as kids. Numb and dumb. He said most of the people who came into the antique shop in Malibu were numb and dumb from too much sun and television and drugs. And art apparently.

My father turned out to be quite an ass in his later years.

Marilee stopped going home to visit our parents. Every few months our mom would come up for a weekend visit. She never brought our dad. And the three of us would have dinner at the Cliff House on Saturday night since my mother was accustomed to fine dining, and the beach, and paying too much money for food. She would go to church with my sister Sunday morning. And then she'd go back home to our dad and say nothing of any of it to him.

Those were the years I was closest to Marilee. By the time I was twenty-seven, we had both been in the city three years, and Marilee was showing her art at some of the local galleries. She made a name for herself decoupaging vintage furniture she bought off Craigslist. I think it was her way of sticking it to our dear old dad—the antiques collector—defacing all those valuable antiques with old newspapers and magazines and turning them into Novocain for fools.

In 2008 she collected thousands of clippings from President Obama's election and completely swathed an army of antique lawn jockeys in them. That was the first piece that won her some critical attention. And after the earthquake in Haiti, she wallpapered a six-foot-tall American Girl dollhouse with images of crumbling homes and disfigured Taíno children. Suddenly galleries all over the country were calling her.

It was about that time that she took our mother's maiden name, having completely fallen out with our father.

She called herself Marilee Lorenzo.

People magazine just ran a story about Marilee last week

anticipating the fortieth anniversary of her death. It mentions me briefly, saying that I recently attended a banquet in my honor at the Lawrence Hall of Science in Berkeley, California, for my work on the SHEM Project.

The article mentioned nothing of my father, the antiques dealer from Minnesota.

The article in *People* said that when Marilee found out she had Lou Gehrig's disease, she flew down to Haiti to join the relief efforts with the American Red Cross. It's a misprint because I know for a fact that Marilee didn't find out she had Lou Gehrig's disease until later. She flew down to Haiti because that was where things really mattered at the time, and Marilee always wanted to be where things mattered most.

When her art took off, Marilee fell into a state of depression. She couldn't stand the idea of people all over the country looking at those gruesome images on the kitchen walls of her American Girl dollhouse and applauding her for being socially conscious.

She lamented in private that she knew she hadn't actually done anything to help.

So while her exhibit toured the country, starting in Los Angeles, where my father refused to see it, and then on to

Austin, then Chicago, and finally ending up in New York, Marilee was in Port-au-Prince lifting cinder blocks off mangled bodies.

At the end of June, just after my fourth anniversary working at Happy Happy Happy Message Runners, Inc., at which I was making about $75,000 a year, I got a letter from Marilee.

The letter wasn't in her handwriting, except for the address on the front of the envelope. It was the scrawl of a child, no more than ten or eleven years old. This is what it said:

Dear Monsieur Frost,

I am writing to tell you today is my birthday. I am going to my father to take me to buy the fish. Tell Kobe Bryant hello please for me.

Emmanuel Blanc

There was also a photograph of Emmanuel Blanc taken on my sister's old Polaroid camera, which had belonged to our mother. The small boy was standing in a churchyard wearing a Lakers jersey with the number twenty-four.

That was the beginning of a stream of letters I would receive from people all over the stricken country. Never once did my sister explain why they were writing to me. And never once did the letters mention anything about the earthquake or the death toll or the turmoil we were seeing all over CNN. I think that was Marilee's point. People can get through just about anything.

I saved the letters and the photographs, and they were later published in a book called *Letters to Jim*, which brought my sister posthumous fame. That was what the article in *People* was mostly about. That and my sister's canonization by the Catholic Church.

CHAPTER 7

I CAME HOME from the hardware store this afternoon to find Eliza in my kitchen. I forgot to call her this morning, so she decided to stop by the house to see if I was dead.

"Maybe I should call Dr. Haug to see if we can get your appointment moved up," she said.

She was, of course, referring to the microchip.

"Then do I have your permission to die?" I asked.

She did not like that one bit.

She asked me where I had been all morning, why I didn't have my cell phone with me at the hardware store.

My cell phone was dead, I explained. Finished. Kaput.

But at least *I* was alive! I reminded her.

She frowned. I never knew a woman who could frown so well. I think she inherited it from my grandfather on my mother's side. I never met the man. He was a big old Sicilian with a frown that made him look like a ventriloquist's dummy.

I explained that the water pressure in my shower was low and that I had gone out to pick up one of those showerheads that gives you a shiatsu massage while you shower.

"I could have picked that up for you," she said.

"I am perfectly capable of doing it myself," I replied.

"Did you see the article about Auntie Marilee in *People*?"

"Yes."

"Did they let you proof it before they ran it?" she asked.

"It wasn't about me," I replied.

"They mentioned you."

"Yes, but I'm not the one with the halo."

"You deserve more recognition," she said. "You're not going to be around much longer."

I'm not sure how things sound to Eliza in her own head, but I certainly know how they sound to me in mine. So I changed the subject and asked her to help me with the new showerhead.

Incidentally, while we were working side by side in the small upright shower unit, she asked me about my grand-father on my mother's side, the one with the marvelous frown. Pasquale Lorenzo. She had stumbled across an old picture of him in a photo album my mother kept, which was passed on to me, and which recently found its way into Eliza's garage with a dozen old boxes I wanted to throw away but that Eliza had insisted on keeping.

Eliza is a hoarder. Not the kind that fills her bathtub with old milk cartons and dead cats, but the kind that cannot seem to let go of sentimental knickknacks, like teddy bears and jewelry and magazine clippings. It might be the *only* way in which Eliza is sentimental.

My mother grew up in Pompeii, Italy, on the beach. Her father was a fashion wholesaler, and when my mother turned fifteen, old Pasquale-with-the-Frown took her to Milan to introduce her to a few modeling agencies, all of which were eager to sign her. She was very beautiful. And her father was very powerful.

She modeled in Milan for several years, until she met my dad, who whisked her away to California like a modern-day Pocahontas.

Eliza, my daughter, wanted to know how Anita, my mother, felt living her whole life an ocean apart from her family.

I can't say I know how my mother felt. My mother never talked about it. But she kept photo albums. Lots and lots of photo albums. After my mother gave up modeling to marry my father, she became something of an amateur photographer. *Snap-snap!*

Eliza wanted to know if we had any family still living in Pompeii or Milan or thereabouts.

Questions, questions!

"Nobody in Italy that I have anything to do with," I told her. "But you have an uncle in Belgium from your mother's side, Duncan."

The last time I mentioned Greta's brother in Antwerp was forty years ago, when I went out there to scatter Greta's ashes on his little farm.

"Is he still alive?" she asked.

"He is indeed still alive, and he's quite a bit older than I am. I think he must be about eighty-three."

Eighty-three is nothing nowadays. Europeans have the longest life-spans in the world. It has something to do with their diets and walking everywhere and the air quality and the general availability of health care over there, which pretty much nobody can get over here anymore.

As a matter of fact, I just got a letter from Duncan Van Bruggen. He tells me he is fine. The weather is colder in Belgium than it was when he was a kid, and the frost has killed his herb garden.

DO NOT RESUSCITATE

These are the types of things he typically shares with me. I wrote him back.

Duncan,

I am doing well here, but your niece Eliza thinks I am dying. The weather in San Francisco is mild, as always. We are having the warmest winter on record. You should try rosemary for your garden. It is very sturdy and usually survives the frost.

J. Frost

We are both lonely old men, so this kind of correspondence is good for us.

Duncan never married. He has lived on the farm his whole life and takes care of the place all on his own. He is healthy and strong and runs a tight ship. Or at least that was how I found him when I visited in December of 2025.

The urn containing my wife's ashes, which had been misplaced by the airline, ended up in Aruba. The people at Queen Beatrix International Airport found it circulating the luggage carousel Christmas morning.

Merry Christmas!

I spent Christmas Day in the Brussels Airport awaiting the return flight from Aruba that was bringing my late wife back from her postmortem vacation. Then I took the train from Brussels to Antwerp, and a taxi from there to the little cottage where Duncan lives. It was past midnight when I arrived. Duncan walked down to meet me at the gate. He led me through a garden covered in freshly fallen snow to the house where he and Greta had grown up together.

The inside of the cottage was orderly and quaint, and had the untouched feeling of a museum, except for the kitchen, which looked lived-in, and where I imagined Duncan spent most of his time.

He served me soup and bread, which I later learned were made from the bounty of his own garden, and he hardly spoke a word except to say that he was sorry I had so much trouble at the airport.

We sat in silence for some time, he on one end of a wooden bench, looking into the fire, and I on the other, staring into my soup. I did not know then if I should take the ashes out of my luggage to share with him—if he wanted to see them or to hold them—or if that would be unsettling. I wondered if he felt any ownership over Greta's ashes, like I did. It was his DNA, not mine, in there, after all.

But because he said nothing, and because I was not in the mood to broach the subject, I decided to put the topic off until morning, and I brought the ashes to my room, where they spent the night with my socks and underwear at the foot of my bed.

The next day we scattered the ashes without much ceremony. I followed Duncan out to a small orchard, which was stripped of all its leaves. The farm was no more than a few acres of fruit trees and vegetable patches, a chicken coop, a hog, and a goat. Not to mention a host of crows, which sat perched on a single telephone wire that ran from the cottage to the road, perhaps the only link between Duncan and the outside world.

I asked Duncan how he thought it should be done.

He took off his gloves and stuck a hand in the urn and pulled out a handful of ashes, the remains of my late wife, his late sister. Then he just dropped it onto the ground.

The ash was gristly and coarse, not like I had imagined it would be, and it turned quickly to mud in the snow. We walked around the yard, tossing it about as if we were feeding chickens.

"That's all of her," he said finally.

"That's all of her," I replied, because I could not think of how else to end our little ceremony.

Back inside the house, Duncan rinsed the urn in an old wooden washbasin and placed it on the windowsill to dry. I didn't want it anymore, the urn, and I told him so.

"I'll bury it in the yard when the ground thaws," he said.

I was satisfied with that solution.

Eliza has always held it against me—my not bringing the urn home for safekeeping. She wishes I had kept it. With no grave site and no urn, she says she has nowhere to *mourn*.

I prefer it that way.

Eliza has already cleared a spot on her mantel for my remains. She showed it to me once and said, "See, this is the proper place to put an urn. Not in the ground with the worms."

She doesn't know it yet, but I have made Spencer the executor of my will, and I'm going to be scattered across AT&T Park. My urn will be smashed to smithereens against the side of a newly christened sailboat. Spencer sails, and he owns lots of boats. He also owns the San Francisco Giants. How's that for making it big?

Eliza can mourn over the titanium canister with the microchip containing my backup brain at Humanity Co.

CHAPTER 8

I JUST RECEIVED an e-mail today from the man in the yellow coat, my new friend, George Ainsley. He has informed me that the Genova Delicatessen is out of business. Finished. Gone. Kaput. It is now a Chinese-run nail salon.

We are still planning to have lunch. And play chess, he says.

I haven't played chess in years. I was an online champ once, in college, during midterms of my freshman year. My dorm had an online chess tournament every term during exams. It was our way of putting off studying until the very last minute.

Charlie was the one who got me into it. He lived two doors down in 501, which was the largest suite on the floor. Charlie had a poker table in there, and a chessboard, and darts. Charlie was very popular on move-in day because he had so many great games that the fellas could sit around and play without having to say too much about themselves. He also had the best hash.

Charlie also had the best girlfriend. Kate Drummond. She was a knockout. She was a year older than we were, and she was studying marine biology. Whenever she came over, she tried to fill our heads with hoopla about the impending apocalypse: the arctic poles melting into the sea, shifting sea currents, a European ice age, invasive species killing off all the indigenous life in the ocean. That sort of thing.

She was pretty much right on the money, it turns out.

I had the hots for Kate Drummond, and Charlie knew it. And he would endlessly taunt me by grabbing her ass and reaching into her crotch in public.

"Wish you had some of this, Frosty?" he would say.

Charlie had a bit of a complex. It was called treating women like shit.

Kate shrugged it off, since she had a complex of her own. It was called not feeling worth anything.

She told me once that she felt helpless, that she always got caught up thinking about all the different decisions a person can make in his or her lifetime, and where all those different decisions lead, and how unpredictable it all is—and a sort of paralysis would come over her. And so she'd just light a joint and fuck around with Charlie because she felt so completely and utterly *helpless.*

She told me this one day after she'd spent the afternoon fucking around with me.

Kate Drummond was right on the money again, I think. We are completely and utterly helpless.

Kate never cheated on Charlie. They were broken up three years before she and I got together. And by that time, Charlie was married to a girl from South Korea.

We had all graduated from Berkeley, and I had moved to the city with my Happy Happy Happy Message Runners, Inc. money. Charlie had quit the museum job and had gone off to South Korea to teach English to second graders, and I had nobody to smoke with anymore. So I called up the closest thing to Charlie I could think of, which was his ex-girlfriend and my longtime crush, Kate Drummond.

Kate was working at Philz Coffee in the Mission District with the rest of the hipsters while she applied to grad school. I don't think she ever ended up going to grad school, but I can't be sure since we lost touch years ago. She loved living in that part of the city because everybody was supposedly very environmentally conscious. San Francisco had ordinances for all sorts of things, like mandatory composting and community gardens and bagless grocery stores.

Lot of good that did anyone. San Francisco was just one city out of thousands. A molehill on Mount Everest. Whoever said one person can make all the difference didn't live in a world with seven billion people.

Today you simply can't afford to live like we were doing back then. We call those years the Age of Innocence. Wikipedia refers to the Age of Innocence as "the period in American history between the end of the Gulf War in 1991 and the California Water Crisis in 2034, when the people of America enjoyed unlimited access to affordable resources like gasoline, water, precious metals, lumber, and food."

They call it the Age of Innocence because they think we didn't know what we were doing back then, so we couldn't possibly be held accountable for our actions.

That's a nice way of putting it.

CHAPTER 9

THE WOMAN who cleans my house just came in, so I have to move out to the living room while she puts the kitchen in order. Then I'll have to move into the bedroom while she puts the living room in order, and then I'll move back into the kitchen once the floors have dried. It's our Sunday routine.

Her name is Pilar Rochac, and she is from El Salvador. Eliza hired Pilar to come into my house and shoo me from room to room. In between subsequent shooings, Pilar cleans the house.

Eliza also hired a gardener to mow my lawn every Tuesday, and somebody to wash my windows, and somebody to launder my shirts. Eliza thinks I am too old to take care of myself, and so she has hired somebody for everything, effectively stripping an old man of his last and only reason for living: to clean up after himself.

And with all the cleaners and washers and gardeners coming and going nowadays, she says she can take comfort in knowing that when I die, somebody will be there to find my corpse.

It's my own doing, all these comings and goings. I gave Eliza free license to manage my estate, mainly because I have more money than I can spend in my lifetime, and there are a lot of people out there who could use some of it. I like to think I'm *fueling the economy*.

The expression "fueling the economy" comes from the early part of the century, when the economy tanked. About the same time I moved into the city. And about the same time Marilee quit her job at Wells Fargo. Everybody thought my sister was crazy for giving up a six-figure salary and benefits during a recession. To go to art school.

"Dead in the water," my dad said of Marilee when he found out. "Your sister is Dead. In. The. Water."

Turns out she was going to be dead either way, but it wasn't the economy nor the Novocain for fools that would kill her. It was Lou Gehrig's disease.

That was about 2008, I think, right about the time Kate

Drummond and I broke off whatever it was we had going on. Kate couldn't afford to live in the city anymore, and both of us knew we weren't serious, so we split up, and she went to live with her parents in Daly City, and I crossed my fingers that the recession wouldn't slow the traffic of mysterious red coolers that were paying for my ninety-inch flat-screen and my Blu-ray player and my Victorian-style townhouse in Hayes Valley.

About that time I got a letter from Charlie. He had moved with his new wife to London, where they were both returning to school, he for a PhD in philosophy and she for a master's in public policy. Old Charlie was finally getting his shit together.

He wrote letters, Charlie, up until he died. He could have e-mailed or iMessaged or FaceTimed from London for no charge. But Charlie preferred to send handwritten letters with eighty-seven-pence Mark Rothko stamps.

Mark Rothko was a Russian-American painter who was famous for painting blocks of color on canvas. Novocain for fools.

At some point in his life, Charlie got his hands on an original Mark Rothko, which he later bequeathed to me in his will, and which now hangs in the living room where Pilar Rochac is dusting.

Charlie's letter wanted to know what I was up to and how I was doing and if I wanted to visit him and his wife, Soo Yeon, in London sometime.

I wrote him back that I was doing fine and that the deliveries business was booming and that I would fly to London if I ever got some time off work.

And as fortune would have it, in February of 2009, right around my twenty-sixth birthday, I got a notice from Happy Happy Happy Message Runners, Inc. saying that all deliveries would be suspended until further notice.

I took this to mean I was out of the job.

I had some money put away, and I figured the best time to travel was between jobs. So I renewed my passport and took Charlie up on his offer.

I flew to London for Christmas that year and crashed on the living room couch in Charlie's flat for a few weeks. Old Charlie had changed. He didn't smoke anymore, or drink for that matter. Soo Yeon didn't allow it. He wore skinny ties and blazers and checkered pants, and I swear I could hear the slant of an English accent when he spoke.

Old Charlie had become the thing he always dreaded becoming: a yuppie.

Soo Yeon had him by the balls. Her English was perfect, and I could tell right away that she was smarter than both

Charlie and I put together. She spent her days in the flat typity-typing away at her master's thesis while Charlie was away in class.

While I was staying with them, I usually woke up late. Charlie would have already left for class, and Soo Yeon would be plugging away on her laptop. So I spent the mornings in London sitting on the couch, browsing for jobs online.

In the afternoons, Soo Yeon prepared glass noodles or kimchi or soup, and we'd sit at the kitchen table and eat together. Then she'd start back on her thesis, and I would go out to wander the streets and take in the sights. I'd swing by the London School of Economics around four, and together Charlie and I would tube home.

I wasn't having any luck in the job search, mainly because I'd spent the past few years working for a nonexistent company as a delivery boy. And so on the cusp of my twenty-seventh birthday, my résumé was about as empty as my bank account.

Then on January 12, 2010, two things happened: an earthquake of magnitude 7.0 hit off the coast of Haiti, and I got an e-mail from Happy Happy Happy Message Runners, Inc. requesting a pickup at the Oakland International Airport the following week.

My funds were running low, and I couldn't afford to miss out on an opportunity to make some cash, so I booked a flight home the next day.

Marilee was looking after my apartment while I was away. When I came home, I found the whole living room cleared out, and standing where my coffee table should have been was a six-foot American Girl dollhouse.

Marilee wasn't home, so I made myself a grilled cheese sandwich and turned on the news. Every station was covering the devastation in Haiti. Fallen buildings. Bloody children. Mass chaos and looting. But it couldn't have seemed farther away to me. Like news from the moon or another star.

The news was having a completely different effect on my sister, it turned out. She came home that evening with a copy of every publication in the city covering the quake.

That was how it started for Marilee: a morbid obsession with suffering that would inflect every decision she would ever make from that point on.

The media later called Marilee's impulse to surround herself with suffering a virtue. I called it a hobby.

Marilee was interested in suffering the way other people are interested in home decor or French cuisine or Frisbee golf. This hobby of hers, coupled with the fact that she happened to be a devout Catholic, are the reasons she is known as *Saint* Marilee Lorenzo today.

That fated day in January of 2010, Marilee Lorenzo began work on the lifelong project that would put her on a collision course with canonization. And I, her good-for-nothing brother, started back at Happy Happy Happy Message Runners, Inc. delivering unscrupulous packages to strangers in delis for cold hard cash.

CHAPTER 10

PILAR ROCHAC has kicked me out of my own house. Today I write from a folding chair on my patio, watching some person I don't even know wash my windows. It amazes me that we have come to this: a person who specializes in mopping floors, and another who specializes in washing windows, and another who mows lawns, and yet another who balances finances, and another who calculates risk, and so on. We are each a cog in some giant cuckoo clock, one man among many in a Fordist assembly line.

And to think in pioneer times most people managed all of it on their own: the floor mopping, the window washing, the lawn mowing, the checkbook balancing, the risk calculating, et cetera.

I sometimes wonder what would happen if all the gardeners or accountants or risk consultants disappeared from the world. People would have to start thinking for themselves again; that's what would happen.

Case in point: I almost got run over the other day crossing the street in front of the bank. I move about as fast as an ice floe, and the light changed color while I was still in the intersection. And this roly-poly of a man stepped on the gas, as if green means go no matter what. And then he saw me and slammed on the brakes and gave me a look as if to say, "You're holding up the assembly line, Jack!" This man would rather a little green light tell him what to do next than think for himself.

I have just had a party to celebrate my seventy-third birthday, and the yard is still littered with plastic cups and cigarette butts and God knows what else. But not to worry, Eliza assures me, Manuel the gardener will clean it up.

All three of my children made it out for the party: Kendra Ann and her husband, Pradip, and their two boys all the way from London; Spencer and Eugene and their two girls out of New York; and of course Eliza and her three girls and a lot of other people I don't have any interest in going on about now, as I had little interest in them last night.

They are all gone now, except for Kendra Ann. She is

staying another week to visit some friends in the area. She is out with a gal now who used to be our neighbor. Jackie Olsen From Next Door, we called her. She became a hotel real estate broker in the city. She recently sold the Sir Francis Drake to a company in China. The Chinese own all the hotels now.

Yesterday Kendra Ann's boys flew back to London with their father. Her eldest, Gokul, is fourteen and managed the flight well enough. The little one, Rajiv, is ten and has been diagnosed with ADHD. But they have all sorts of digital entertainment on flights now with which to anesthetize the young. Kendra Ann reports that Rajiv managed just fine, too.

When she isn't out with her girlfriends, Kendra Ann sits on the couch and reads while I write. She reads mystery novels, like her mother used to do, and she has managed to dig up an old collection of Janet Evanovich novels from the basement. They start *One for the Money* and *Two for the Dough*. The series goes on like that, *Three to Get Deadly* and *Four to Score* and so on.

I, myself, prefer nonfiction. I have enough trouble wrapping my head around all the things that have actually happened on this planet. I don't have time to worry about all the things that happen in other people's imaginations.

Tonight Kendra Ann wants to take me OOTT. Translation: out on the town. She noted, quite accurately, that I haven't left the house in days. I usually get out a lot more, I told her. I like to go for walks in the park across the street. But lately there has been a woman there whom I am trying to avoid. Her name is Eleanor Summerland. She is a widow. And she thinks it would be a grand idea for she and I to get married.

Naturally, I asked, WTHF? In Eleanor's native tongue, that means "what the hell for?"

For creature comforts, she said.

I couldn't tell whether she meant money or sex. But from what I can tell, she has plenty of money. Her husband left her the deed to a private groundwater supply in Marin County. Might as well have struck oil! And as for sex— that'd be like asking me to do a cartwheel on a balance beam.

So I am avoiding the park until she goes away or dies. She is pushing ninety. Won't be long now.

Unless she has a microchip. Eliza says it is going to be the elixir of life. "Just think of it!" she says. "When they figure out the technology, someday after you're dead, you'll suddenly wake up in a young person's body, maybe even your own, and you'll be able to go on living again!"

Magnum Opus!

I shudder to think of it. Maybe Eliza is too young to understand this, but I am just about done. Finished. Kaput.

Kendra Ann knows better than to bring up this microchip business. Instead she tells me she is taking me to a basketball game at the high school tonight. Her old coach got in touch with her recently, and he wants Kendra Ann to see the team play while she's in town. He says that they've still got her photograph on display in a trophy case in the gym lobby. Kendra Ann was the high school league MVP three years running. She was recruited by the San Francisco State Gators, and she was the star player there, too.

Then she was recruited by the WNBA, and she wound up playing for the L.A. Sparks. But she sat on the bench most of the time. Not to mention she got knocked up midway through her first season. So she quit the Big League and moved home.

Kendra Ann is about six-four. She gets it from her mother's side of the family. There are some real whoppers in the Van Bruggen family tree. I'm told my father-in-law was seven feet tall. He died of heart complications before Greta was old enough to have any memory of him. They say his corpse wouldn't fit into an ordinary casket, so they had to bury him in a horse crate, and the makeshift casket had to be interred perpendicular to the grave site, spanning two burial plots, since it wouldn't have fit otherwise.

When Duncan and I paid a visit to his grave during my stay in Antwerp, Duncan said when you sit facing the headstone, you're facing his father's hip. So it is better to look west toward his head. I don't really see what difference it makes which part of his dead father I'm facing.

Duncan isn't particularly tall. Maybe six-two. And Greta wasn't either. Their father, whom I'm told was a veritable yeti of a man, ran the family farm, which at the time spanned about a thousand acres of wetlands popular for grazing sheep. But after the old man died, Greta's mother parceled out the land to the neighboring farmers for 4,000 Belgian francs an acre. She kept only the main house and the surrounding forty acres for herself and her two children.

The whole region turned out to be the site of a major freshwater aquifer, and the land is now valued at about a quarter million US dollars an acre.

Duncan inherited the farm when his mother died. He planted the apple orchard, since the climate of Belgium is better suited for apples now. He planted hedgerows around the property to keep out the neighbors' sheep. And he installed an electric pump for easy access to his gold mine of water. He refuses to sell the land, however, even though the state has offered him twice its going value.

People everywhere are willing to pay a lot of money for water.

It is a thirsty, thirsty world.

Greta left her father's farm to attend university in Paris in 2001, when she was only fifteen. She was the youngest student in her class, and earned the highest marks, even though French was not her native language. She entered Pierre and Marie Curie University as a classics major, studying Greek and Latin and ancient philosophy. But she was steadily lured away by the sciences, which seemed to have more convincing answers to the questions that plagued her. Where do we come from? Where are we going? What's the point of it all?

She was satisfied with the explanation that we are all made up of the stuff of ancient suns and that we have the fiery furnaces of dying stars to thank for all the elements on the periodic table. She agreed that only the strongest and quickest and smartest survive. And she understood that humans were turning our planet into a shithole of greenhouse emissions and nuclear waste.

There was a professor of biology at the university by the

name of Gerard Boule who took an interest in young Greta Van Bruggen. He offered her an internship with his research group. After four months of working closely with Greta in the lab, he whisked her away to Indonesia to spend the summer studying endemic island plants.

They carried all of their equipment on their backs. They slept in a single tent. They bartered with local merchants for food and supplies. Greta spoke Dutch, French, and English fluently, which came in handy since the islands were a patchwork of dissolved colonies from all parts of Europe.

Each day they staked out a five-hundred-square-meter parcel of land and combed through every inch looking for rare varieties of trees or shrubs native to Indonesia. The location of every specimen was logged in a computer database, and from it, they were able to produce a digital map of the country showing the growth patterns of rare and exotic species.

Some plants preferred sunny, temperate westward-facing shores, while others survived best in the windswept plains of dried-up river basins. Some occupied regions no larger than a backyard, while others traced long, winding webs across the archipelago. Each plant had its own unique growth pattern, which gave hints as to what exactly these rare plants needed to survive.

Many of the plants were on the verge of extinction and were numbered among the last of their kind. With the map they were making, Gerard Boule and young Greta Van Bruggen were able to advise the Indonesian government on the best places to designate national parks and conservation sites.

It was sometime in the midst of this adventure that sixteen-year-old Greta Van Bruggen became pregnant.

Greta went to see a medicine woman in the village where they were staying. Her name was Rasima Rasima. Rasima Rasima prescribed an herbal blend of nutmeg and papaya, believed to have abortifacient properties. This was supplemented by a deep abdominal massage.

Two months into the pregnancy, Greta miscarried.

She never told Boule about the pregnancy. He had a wife and three kids of his own back in Paris. Surely Madame Boule had her suspicions about Greta, but the understanding seemed to be that as long as Boule came home to his family at the end of the summer, nobody needed to be the wiser.

Rasima Rasima was sympathetic.

"I see your future," she said to Greta. "You will have many children. And your children will have many children. But this child was never yours to keep. God has other plans for you."

I don't know about God, but Happy Happy Happy Message Runners, Inc. certainly had other plans for Greta Van Bruggen.

When they got back to Paris at the end of summer, Greta politely resigned from Boule's research team and went to work at the Jardin des Plantes, a seventy-acre botanical garden in the fifth arrondissement, across the street from the university.

She had a few other boyfriends back then, guys her own age, and they took her to the cinema and to wine bars and salsa dancing, feeble attempts at sophistication. And although none of these boys had any of the spark or charm of Gerard Boule, she found their amateur overtures refreshing. And she never went farther than second base with any of them. And word around school was that Greta Van Bruggen was a prude and a square.

Duncan visited her once in 2004. He was still working on the farm in Antwerp, and it was the farthest he had ever been from home. Greta put him on the couch in the living room of the two-bedroom apartment she and three girlfriends were sharing on rue Mandar in the second arrondissement, a few blocks from the Louvre. The way Greta used to tell the story, Duncan never left the apartment except to visit her at the Jardin des Plantes, where he made friends with all the botanists. Then he went home and never visited Paris or anywhere else ever again.

Duncan knows all about Gerard Boule and Rasima Rasima and the abortion. Greta told her brother in the strictest confidence. As far as I can tell, he didn't love her one ounce less for any of it. Who would? She was the most wonderful woman in the world.

CHAPTER 11

INCIDENTALLY, Rasima Rasima, the medicine woman whom Greta consulted in Indonesia, would later serve as a trusted consultant to my late sister Marilee Lorenzo. Rasima Rasima and Marilee met at a field hospital in Port-au-Prince, Haiti, after the earthquake in 2010.

The Red Cross volunteers stayed in tents, and ate around a portable stove, and relied heavily on relief shipments from all around the world for their food and clothing and supplies.

Marilee wrote to me from their camp on May 7, 2010. I have kept the letter all these years, and I will transcribe it here.

Dear Jim,

There is so much I have to tell you. The people here are

remarkable. So many of them have lost someone they love: a family member, a neighbor, a friend. But there is something in the air here, a sort of brotherhood. People are coming together from all over the world to help, and it's like nothing I've ever experienced. So many of the people here are asking, "Why would God let this happen?" But I look around and see that God has given us an opportunity to do his work.

I know what you'd say to that. You'd say phooey. Things just happen. There doesn't have to be a reason. Nobody cares what we do on this planet. And when we die, we're dead. Finished. Kaput. That's what you'd say, right?

I don't think so.

I am living in a Red Cross field camp, and every night there is a group of us who get together to pray. We pray for the people who are suffering here. Sometimes we pray for the people back home, too. I know you don't care much for praying, but it's my way of coping with the unfathomable world around me. And sometimes it is the only thing I can do when we've run out of clean bandages or water or food.

There is a woman from Indonesia who comes to our prayer group. She is old, maybe sixty or seventy, and she cares for patients at the hospital. She doesn't wince at the sight of blood. If a patient is missing an arm or a leg or an eye, she doesn't even flinch. Her name is Rasima Rasima, but she calls herself Sister Rosemary.

I asked her how she stays so calm when people all around her are dying. She says she has been a medicine woman her whole life, and her mother was a medicine woman, and her mother's mother before that. In her house growing up, there was always suffering. She says home is a place where people go to suffer and die, and she feels at home here.

I wish I could feel that way, too. I think if I could see things that way, then I could begin to be of some use to somebody.

Missing you always,
Marilee

That was the only letter I ever got from Marilee written in her own hand. The rest of the letters came from children, and only the envelopes were addressed in Marilee's familiar scrawl.

"Dear Jim," one letter said, "Sister Marilee says you went to Berkeley. I want to go to Berkeley someday. Aaron Rodgers went to Berkeley. They say only the smartest people in the world go there. You must be really smart. I am getting all As, and hopefully I will go there, too."

The letter was signed, "Barthélemy DuPont, Age 13."

"Sister Marilee is an angel," one little girl wrote.

And one boy wrote, "Sister Marilee is FAMOUS!"

It was true. My sister Marilee had made a name for herself in Port-au-Prince. I didn't know anything about it until, one very hot day in August, I was sitting on the couch with a fan blowing on my face and a cold beer in my hand, and her picture came up on the TV.

She was stepping out of a church in Port-au-Prince, and people everywhere were crowding around her and reaching out to touch her hands. The cameras cut to the Red Cross relief hospital where Marilee was going from patient to patient with a carafe of water.

The news crawl read, "Local Artist Turns Humanitarian."

I finally met Rasima Rasima in San Francisco in 2017 at Marilee's funeral. It was Greta who recognized her first, and she went to Rasima Rasima and clasped her hands warmly and called her by her old name. But Rasima Rasima blinked her eyes and shook her wizened head. She introduced herself as Sister Rosemary, which was the Catholic title she had adopted when she joined the sisterhood, and she apologized because she had seen so many patients in her lifetime she could not remember them all.

We crossed paths again at Marilee's canonization in Rome in 2042. Toward the end of her life, Rasima Rasima looked like a rag doll. She was blind, and she smelled of cumin and garlic and all the other spices that were commonly found in her medicinal teas. She didn't recognize me then, either. She died two years later in a nunnery where she had retired to write the story of Marilee's life.

Rasima Rasima began her book, "I would have traded all the years of my life to give Our Lady Saint Marilee Lorenzo just one more day on this earth. She could do so much in a day; it was as if every precious minute held some latent miracle just waiting for Our Lady to come and wake it up."

Rasima Rasima was not always so devout. When Greta went to her for an abortion in 2002, Rasima Rasima sub-scribed to a conglomeration of mystical and spiritual teach-ings that had been passed down in Indonesian culture for hundreds of years, influenced by Hindu, Islamic, and Protestant practices, and heralding back to a time when the island people attributed both tragedy and fortune to ancestral spirits that resided in rocks and trees and animals.

According to her book, *The Life and Deeds of Our Lady Saint Marilee Lorenzo*, published by HarperCollins in 2044,

Rasima Rasima describes her coming-to-Jesus moment as "a quick smack on the face, the way my mother used to do when we misbehaved." The epiphany came while she and her sister and a neighbor were sitting together on the porch smoking opium and kecubung.

Rasima Rasima claims Jesus came to her in a vision, on Rollerblades, and told her to go to the mission in the nearby village for an ultrasound.

She asked Jesus whatever for.

Jesus reportedly said, "So you can see for yourself all the little dead babies rotting in your belly, conceived by your sin."

Rasima Rasima knew what Rollerblades were because her nephew wore them to deliver newspapers in the village. And she was familiar with the mission in the nearby village because she passed it often on the way to the market. And she knew what an ultrasound was because several of the women she helped miscarry had brought in fuzzy black-and-white pictures as proof of purchase, so to speak.

When Rasima Rasima passed the mission the following Sunday, the Red Cross was stationed out front recruiting volunteers to help with the relief efforts in Haiti. She had not heard about the earthquake in Haiti until that very moment, but she wondered if Jesus had meant for this to be her path to

God. So she signed up.

My sister, as I already mentioned, was obsessed with suffering. And she had already found Jesus. So she signed up to help out with the relief efforts, too, coincidentally, at a free clinic in the Mission District in San Francisco.

Their paths would soon collide. "God's will," Rasima Rasima wrote of their meeting in 2010.

"Lucky break," I say.

In her book, Rasima Rasima explains that on the night she dreamed of Jesus on Rollerblades, her sister had a vision, too. It was of penguins on trampolines.

Rasima Rasima knew what a penguin was from grade school. She knew what a trampoline was, too, because her mother used to treat a white woman in the village for headaches, and one day they all went to the white woman's house, where the white children were jumping up and down, up and down on a giant trampoline.

Their neighbor, that night, had a vision of Groucho Marx. Rasima Rasima did not know anything about Groucho Marx. But her neighbor did, apparently.

Incidentally, I have seen an actual penguin on a trampoline in a circus act in Long Beach. It wasn't as remarkable as you'd think.

When Rasima Rasima arrived in Port-au-Prince, straight

off the plane from Indonesia, the chief medical officer in charge of the Red Cross volunteers, a towering Haitian from Saint-Germain who did his medical training in Miami, Florida, misunderstood when Rasima Rasima introduced herself for the first time, and called her Rosemary.

Rasima Rasima took this as God's way of giving her a new Christian name, and so she became Sister Rosemary of Bali, a name that would forever be associated with my sister, Our Lady Saint Marilee Lorenzo of San Francisco.

The theological scholar Thomas A. Rhett recently published a paper in *Bible America* called "The Origins of a Saint: The Quest of Sister Rosemary of Bali for the Canonization of Our Lady Saint Marilee Lorenzo of San Francisco: The Woman behind the Woman."

Rhett describes the part Rasima Rasima played in my sister's sainthood after she died as "a labor laboris, an opus operis, a magnum opus! Rasima Rasima single-handedly assured that the name of Marilee Lorenzo, and in effect, her own name, would endure forever."

It turns out Eliza isn't the first person to try to live forever. And it doesn't necessarily take a microchip, either. There are many paths to immortality.

CHAPTER 12

IT LOOKS LIKE I have a potential agent for my book, an old college buddy who went to law school to study criminal justice and came out a copyright lawyer. No shame in that. When he realized he couldn't hack it at a law firm, even as a copyright lawyer, he became an agent for TV writers in Hollywood.

One of his clients, a guy who wrote for an Emmy Award–winning sci-fi television series for twenty years, just published his first book: a novel. It's about a future where the US president is elected by popular vote on a TV game show called *Pin the Tail on the President*.

The candidates have to complete all sorts of challenges, like eating live slugs and balancing on tightropes and sumo wrestling. There are talent shows, too, and a fashion segment, and interviews with family and friends.

At the end of each episode, the audience at home phones in their votes, and the presidential candidate with the least votes is eliminated from the show.

Sounds an awful lot like the real thing, if you ask me.

Sam Getz is the name of my college buddy who wants to agent my book. I told him what I was doing, writing it all down before I get my brain downloaded onto a microchip, lest something goes wrong, and he said that publishers would kill to get their hands on my autobiography, what with my part in the SHEM Project and my sister the saint and Spencer's recent fame as an energy expert.

I told him I had no intention of publishing, and he just laughed and laughed and laughed.

This is what he said to me when he was finally done laughing: "Look, Jim. A book as important as the one you're about to write always ends up getting published one way or another. Maybe now. Maybe after you're dead. Wouldn't you feel more comfortable if you knew it was in good hands?"

Spoken like a true lawyer.

I was just thinking. It used to be that a decent man, a respectable man, concerned himself his whole life with three important undertakings: finding a good woman to marry, securing a sturdy house to live in, and writing an epitaph for his headstone. But in today's world, it seems a man can get along just fine without ever deciding to do any one of those things, and he can still be called respectable.

Different times, different times.

I made two of those decisions in my life. I married the love of my life, Greta Van Bruggen, and I bought this house here in San Francisco.

I never decided on an epitaph because I am going to be incinerated and made into fertilizer for AT&T Park. Tombstones are expensive, besides.

Spencer did not concern himself with any of those decisions, and I have it on good authority that he doesn't plan to, and Spencer is the most respectable man I know.

Different times, different times.

I made the first of these so-called important decisions in 2010, when I was twenty-seven. That was also the time my world got turned on its head. Marilee had gone off to Haiti, and was making headlines for her work with the Red Cross and for her decoupaged dollhouse, which was touring the country and getting rave reviews from plebeians and art critics alike. I was all alone in San Francisco with my flat-screen TV and high-speed Internet and cheap-as-hell water, and I guess that's why I decided buying a house was the logical next step. I didn't have much else to do with all that money.

And back then, buying a house, especially a big house with a big yard and lots and lots of green, green grass in constant need of cheap-as-hell water, well, that was respectable.

Not today, not today.

I had just closed on a little two-bedroom on Ortega, big enough for me and my flat-screen TV and whatever else I wanted, when I got another e-mail from Happy Happy Happy Message Runners, Inc. that said I had a pickup at the San Francisco International Airport for someone by the name of "Logan Wallace."

Okeydokey.

But when I got to the airport, I waited and waited, and the red cooler never appeared. I asked the personnel there if Delta Air Lines flight 2245 had arrived. Yes, it had. I asked if all the luggage for flight 2245 had been unloaded. Yes, it had. I asked if there was possibly some mistake, because my luggage wasn't there.

And then they asked me what my name was, if I had the baggage claim ticket, et cetera, et cetera.

No, no, I said.

I told them some story that I had gone over many times in my head for cases just like these. I told them I was picking up the bag for my friend Logan Wallace, who had been on the plane but had caught the first cab to the hospital because of a family emergency. I was a family friend.

I had another story, too, that I had thought up for cases just like these. Want to hear it? Here goes: I was picking up a bag for Logan Wallace, who had checked his luggage but had managed last-minute to catch an earlier flight to San Jose. He had asked me to retrieve his luggage from San Francisco International since he lived in San Jose and I lived in the city. I was his personal assistant or some other such thing.

But I didn't use that one, in case they looked up Logan Wallace in their system and found he had not, in fact, caught an earlier flight to San Jose.

I had one more alibi at the ready. Want to hear it? Here goes: I was picking up a bag for Logan Wallace. He had checked his luggage at the airport but had somehow missed his flight. He had asked me to retrieve the bag and keep it safe until he arrived.

But that one wouldn't work if there was a real Logan Wallace and the flight manifest showed him getting on to the plane.

So because I had no idea if Logan Wallace, or any of the other names I had been given over the years, were real people that actually got on to planes or not, I went with the first alibi.

Logan Wallace was on the plane, but he had to rush to the hospital, so there I was to retrieve his luggage.

"Logan Wallace," said the pretty Delta Air Lines representative at the main kiosk. "I see a booking for a Logan Wallace on flight two-two-four-five. But it looks like he never boarded the plane."

"Are you sure?" I said. "Could you check again, please?"

Stalling. I had to think of something. Hadn't I just said that Logan Wallace had arrived and had rushed off to the hospital?

"I'm certain," said the representative. She scanned through her records again. "Maybe he missed a connection in Chicago."

"Come to think of it," I said, "I haven't heard from him today. I suppose he could have missed his connection. We haven't spoken since we made plans for me to pick up his luggage."

Like a pro. Like a pro.

"Aha! Here it is," the pretty representative said. "Logan Wallace checked in for flight three-nine-eight-two from

Seoul to Chicago with one bag, but the flight was canceled just before takeoff due to mechanical difficulties."

She looked up at me and added, "So that explains why he didn't make his connection in Chicago."

"Was he put on another flight?" I asked.

"He's nowhere else in the system," she said.

"So what happened to his luggage?"

"He must have picked it up at the baggage claim in Seoul." She shrugged a little shrug.

She reminded me of Kate Drummond, Charlie's ex. My ex. Except Kate Drummond had a tattoo of an eagle on the underside of her wrist. This girl only had a watch, which I noticed was still set to daylight savings time even though it was already December.

I wanted to ask her out, and maybe sometime down the road if we were still friends or lovers, I could tell her what a marvelous secret agent I had been the day I met her. I think she would have been impressed.

But as it was, I was scared shitless by my little brush with airport security, and I just wanted out of there.

Remember: I still didn't know what was in those red coolers that I had been delivering for almost five years. I imagined five years' worth of cocaine, or harvested organs from kidnapped children and prostitutes, or God knows what. Enough cocaine and organs and God knows what to land me in the San Quentin State Penitentiary, surely. I should have consulted my friend Sam Getz, who had studied criminal justice at Harvard and was now selling TV scripts out in Hollywood.

But what would Sam Getz know about it? Except how to turn it into a movie. And I'm pretty sure that's what he's trying to do now, all these years later, with the book I'm writing.

When I arrived home from the airport that day, I e-mailed Happy Happy Happy Message Runners, Inc. and explained what had happened, leaving out the part about wanting to ask the Delta Air Lines representative out on a date.

And then I just waited for a reply.

All of my things were still in boxes from the move to the new house, and I was sleeping on a nest of blankets and pillows on the floor in one of the bedrooms because the bed I ordered had not yet arrived.

The reply came three days later, in the mail, just about the same time my bed arrived. I received a manila envelope that was addressed to my old apartment on Hayes Street but which had been forwarded to my new address per my instructions to the post office.

And do you want to know what was in the envelope?

1. A US passport
2. A United Airlines boarding pass
3. A letter from Happy Happy Happy Message Runners, Inc.
4. $2,000 in US cash and three million in South Korean won

First question: Whose US passport could it be?

It was mine! The picture was mine anyway. At first glance, it looked identical to the passport I had renewed last year to visit Charlie in London. Except for one thing.

The name on the passport was Logan Wallace.

The letter explained that there was a flight departing the next day for Seoul, South Korea. I was to assume the identity of Logan Wallace, board the flight using the boarding pass provided, go to Seoul, locate the missing package, which presumably belonged to me, Logan Wallace, and which must still be circulating in the airport somewhere, and then use the three million won to buy a ticket home.

There were specific instructions on how to handle the

package as well, once I had located it. I was not, under any circumstances, to check the package at the terminal. I was to carry it on the plane with me. Upon arrival in San Francisco, I was to deliver it immediately to a man in a Santa suit on the corner of Market and Eighteenth Street.

This was all one week before Christmas.

The $2,000 was a reward for my trouble, as well as compensation for any expenses incurred along the way. I would be rewarded another $8,000 if I returned with the package in tow and handed it off to the man in the Santa suit.

I wanted nothing more than to throw the envelope into my newly restored colonial-style fireplace. But there was one thing that stopped me, one thing that sent my moral compass spinning.

Cold hard cash.

It was a trap. If somebody had asked me to subvert the government and board a plane to another territory under a name that did not belong to me to retrieve a package that did not belong to me, which contained God knows what, I would have, in theory, refused on moral grounds.

In theory.

How many times have humans used those words to paint their own portraits in a better light? "In theory."

In practice, $2,000 is a lot of money, especially when

paired with another $8,000 to make a grand total of $10,000.

That was just enough money to make the needle of the compass, which so steadfastly points north, stand on its head.

What can I say? I had a mortgage to pay.

So I numbed myself with the help of Courtney Love, which was the name of some hash I got over in the Haight. And I packed my bags. And I slept like a log. And I boarded a plane for South Korea the next day.

Why not?

CHAPTER 13

THE HOUSE I live in now has six bedrooms and four and a half baths. An upgrade. And if this were still the Victorian era, the era in which this house was built, a house of this size and stature would surely mark me as a respectable and decent man.

But now a house of this size and stature only means I am using more of the world's resources than I deserve.

I still have the same bed from our old house on Ortega, which I ordered from Robinson Furniture Company all those years ago, a big four-post with a mattress fit for a king. My mother always said, "Never skimp on a bed."

Greta and I sold the house on Ortega and moved into this one when Kendra Ann was born. Kendra Ann spent her whole life in this house, that is, until she moved to Los

Angeles to play for the Sparks and got knocked up.

She just flew home to London yesterday. While she was visiting, she stayed in the same room that she lived in growing up. I still call it Kendra Ann's room, even though she hasn't lived here for at least fifteen years.

We still call this California, even though it's two entirely new states now.

What's in a name?

The house I live in now is a pretty Victorian manor on Gough Street, built circa 1880 and painted a lime green that makes it distinguishable from its neighbors. It stands a few meters above street level on a small grassy mound, which the Chinese say is good chi. Furthermore, the front door opens on Lafayette Park, which a Google satellite image will show as a vibrant green quadrangle bespeckled with scantily clad sunbathers of every make, shape, and creed, basking in the glow of a warm October sun. You can tell it is October because some of the trees are yellow.

Good chi.

I get lost in this house sometimes, in the middle of the night when I can't sleep. I wander the corridors like Marley's ghost, looking in on the silent rooms and thinking of Duncan's small cottage, where he and Greta grew up and which, despite its considerably smaller size, is just as much a museum as my house.

Someday, too, if the microchip really does work, people will wander through the chambers of my mind like Marley's ghost, looking in on the hazy relics of thought and wondering how something that was once so full of life can gather so much dust.

Too bad there isn't a Pilar Rochac for that, too.

I think I will give Pilar Rochac the Mark Rothko when I am gone. Or the Degas, which belonged to Greta.

Much of the furniture in this house we inherited from my father, who left me his antique shop after he died. My mother certainly did not want any of it. Postmenopause, my mother developed a taste for *le moderne*, and she began to look on anything predating the twenty-first century as vile and gruesome, like a corpse.

That might explain her feelings toward my father. After he died, my mother moved out of their quaint 1960s beach house in Malibu, into a chic condo on Point Dume made almost entirely of glass and chrome. She took up golf and tennis and horseback riding at the Point Dume Country Club. She had lunch dates every week with women who were about as well-to-do as she was and who also abhorred anything old or aging because it reminded them of themselves.

She had several friends from Milan and Napoli and Rome, none of whom she knew when she was young, all of whom had been shipped out to Malibu, as she had, by wealthy husbands who had all died, like my father, of stress-induced heart failure, and with whom she spoke exclusively in Italian, elevating her status in the eyes of the other country club women because she was *European*.

What a strange woman she turned out to be!

I think being caged up your whole life with dead people's old things can do that to a person. Like spending your life in a mausoleum. That's what the antique shop felt like to me and my sisters growing up, anyway.

Now those dead people's old things are in my house.

My mother met my father in Milan during Fashion Week, 1975. After the dissolution of Franklin Brothers Used Cars & Parts, my father took a trip to Europe to "see the sights." I think all he really wanted to see were the cars. And the women.

He had lots of money from Franklin Brothers Used Cars & Parts, and he never paid a cent of it to the government.

Like father, like son.

So my father lived it up in Paris and Barcelona and

Greece and Rome. In Milan he went to the runway shows to see the pretty girls, and he ended up coming home with one.

My mother would later tell me and my sister, in a rare vulnerable moment (when she was full to the brim with Cliff House rum runners), that my father was American and rich, and that was enough to satisfy her girlish fantasies and, at the same time, infuriate her own father-with-the-frown, with whom she had always harbored a secret grudge for keeping her out of school to do modeling.

Marilee, of course, suggested my mother go back to school.

"What for?" my mother said. "So I can become a hotshot computer scientist and run around the office on a skateboard, throwing computers down stairs?" She had just seen a documentary on PBS about the young people in the social networking industry.

It turned out what she really wanted to do was take photographs. But nobody knew that until after she died. I found at least twenty photo albums dating back to her days in Pompeii stashed away in the attic of her condo in Malibu.

I do remember her being an avid picture taker when I was a kid. But I thought that was how all mothers were.

What my dad wanted her to be, I think, was a Russian nesting doll, a little wooden doll within a doll within a doll.

What I mean is he wanted her to make lots and lots of babies. And she did. My oldest sister, Emily, was born within a year of their honeymoon. And then came Laura, and Jillian, and Annabel. *Pop, pop, pop!* They took a little breather before I came along, and then Marilee.

I'm the only little wooden doll left.

Heart disease runs in our family. My father died in 2020 from cardiac arrest. Emily and Annabel went out that way, too, in their late fifties. Jillian had a stroke when she was fifty-eight. Laura was luckier: she made it to sixty-three and died in her sleep. There was never an autopsy, but we suspected she died of a pulmonary embolism.

With the exception of Marilee, who was as thin as a flute, all of my sisters were obese. They had my father's genes, old Midwesterner stock, ranchers raised on dairy and beef.

Marilee and I took after our mother, who came from a long line of Sicilian seafarers and fisherfolk, nimble-bodied men and women with severe features and sunken eyes, well-catalogued in the earliest of our mother's photo albums.

Age has only made me thinner (so that Eliza worries all the time that I'm not eating enough), and time has made my ears, nose, and brow more pronounced.

None of my sisters were alive long enough to have their brains downloaded onto microchips.

They are gone forever. Finished. Dead. Kaput.

I don't have any nieces or nephews, either. Marilee died too young and too celibate to have children.

The other four were fat old hens that preferred each other's company to the company of men.

The Four Spinsters Frost, my friend Charlie used to joke.

My older sisters lived their entire lives in Malibu. They were all four of them dental hygienists. They spent the majority of their short, fat lives staring down other people's throats. The one piece of good advice they ever gave me: floss daily.

Incidentally, they say flossing daily cuts down on the risk of heart disease.

Go figure.

When my mother moved into the condo on Point Dume, she bought all new furniture imported from European designers, installed the latest amenities, and picked out a new wardrobe for herself.

Where did she get the money?

My father left behind a sizable fortune, not to mention a prize car collection, which he had kept a secret from the family for forty years, until his death, which occurred on June 18, 2020, behind the sales counter of the antique shop.

He was ringing up a customer, a long-forgotten talk show host and her husband, when he went into cardiac arrest. They say it took all of two minutes, and then it was over. Finished. Dead. Kaput. The whole affair made the ten-o'clock news. "Death of a Salesman," the headlines read. "Famous talk show host left speechless when salesman dies at her feet."

My father left his car collection to my mother in his will. The cars were holed up in warehouses in Victorville, Ventura, and someplace back in Minnesota. There were thirty-eight cars in all, in mint condition, most of them predating the Vietnam War.

We contacted Rick Milliken, dad's old partner from Franklin Brothers Used Cars & Parts, and let him have first pick of the lot for a discounted price, and then we auctioned off the rest, along with the furniture from the antique shop that neither I nor my sisters wanted.

Greta had never seen the antique shop before my father died. We flew down to Los Angeles for the funeral, and stayed a few days to help my mother board up the store, which was her immediate impulse now that my father was gone. The moment Greta stepped inside the musty old mausoleum, she was smitten.

"It's beautiful," Greta said, "like walking back in time."

It was true. My father had a taste for only the most

sophisticated pieces: ornate chests from colonial trade ships, candelabras from post-colonial churches, Winchester rifles in working order, turn-of-the-century glassware from Tiffany's, cutlery from Sheffield, and bejeweled cigarette cases by Fabergé worth up to $30,000 apiece.

Quite a fortune indeed.

And we had our pick of the litter, so to speak. My father left the store and everything in it to me. He stated in his will that if there was anybody in the family who knew how to make money out of manure, it was his son, Jim Frost. I was the only kid of his with any guts, he said. "So to Jim, I leave all my shit."

Thanks, Dad.

Greta wanted to give the house on Gough Street, which we had bought only a few months earlier, an authentic feel, like a real Victorian manor. Thanks to my father, the house was furnished head to toe with rare antiques dating back to the Gilded Age, a time when a house such as this one commanded respect and represented the prosperity of a nation.

Today a house such as this one is "a symbol of our nation's excess and ongoing environmental abuse." At least that is what one young solicitor told me when I opened my door the other day to find a small congregation of protestors on my stoop.

They were from a local coalition called the MOVEment, and they go around to large property owners in San Francisco and try to convince them to move to smaller, more eco-friendly living spaces.

I told them to get the hell off my stoop.

Our house was featured in the March 2021 issue of *BBC Homes and Antiques* magazine, back when the American Dream meant something to hopefuls all over the world.

Today the American Dream is seen for what it always was: a wolf in sheep's clothing.

None of my children want this house when I'm gone, nor do they have any interest in inheriting any of the treasures it holds.

"It's too much upkeep," Eliza says. "And what do I need with a place this size? My kids are practically all grown up."

I have put it in my will that this house and all its contents are to be sold at auction, and the proceeds are to be divided among my seven grandchildren. Pilar Rochac can have the Rothko and Degas. Eliza can have what remains of my father's car collection in Ventura. Spencer will inherit my investments in InfraGen Tech, which are considerable, and Kendra Ann will inherit the savings account, which I opened in 1998, and which is valued at $760,217.67, thanks to prodigious frugality on the part of Greta and myself.

You're welcome.

There are a few pieces in this house that I will donate to the San Francisco Art Institute: a watercolor by the French painter Jean-Baptiste-Camille Corot entitled, *Les Déchus*; a chaise lounge from the apartment of Henrietta Levine, a New York socialite who was tried and hanged for poisoning a US congressman in 1902; a complete collection of the works of Mark Twain signed by the author; a quill pen that belonged to the British stage actor Sir Henry Irving; and a decoupaged bookshelf my sister created for her apartment before her meteoric rise to fame.

I have given these final instructions to a lawyer friend of mine, not Sam Getz who is trying to publish my book, but an actual lawyer named Holly Carter, who defended me during the Lambert-Keaton trials in 2039. She has written my final prattle down in legal terms, airtight, as they say, so that when I'm dead, there won't be any nasty battles over who gets what and so forth.

I have made Spencer the executor of my will.

As for the microchip, for which I still have an appointment in less than a month—well, that opens a whole new can of worms, Holly says.

"Imagine," she said during our last meeting, "if they

develop the technology to upload your brain onto a clone. Well, what then? Who is to act on your behalf then? Your children? Your grandchildren? And who gets to decide when to wake you up, and where, and how, if at all? And then what? Where will you live? How will you make a living?"

She looked grave, more grave than she had ever looked during the Lambert-Keaton trials.

"Consider carefully what you are doing."

Holly is about my age, maybe a little older, and is just about as skeptical as I am about living forever.

"I don't know about you," she said, "but I'm ready to go right now!"

"Me too!" I said.

Done. Finished. Kaput.

In a recent interview with *Time* magazine, I was asked by the correspondent there, a young twentysomething with his mouth agape, if I think human civilization is getting closer to enlightenment.

I said, "About as close as Icarus got to the sun."

Then he wanted to know what was my greatest criticism of the human race.

"That we made wings out of wax," I said.

The article was never published.

NICHOLAS PONTICELLO

Here is the latest from Duncan, dated April 15, 2056:

Hullo Jim,

I planted the rosemary like you suggested, and it is coming along marvelously. If I am not careful, it will take over the whole garden. It is asparagus season here, and the air is perfumed with an earthy aroma, which is produced when the shoots ripen in the ground. My new neighbor has agreed to pay me two euros per kilo for my first harvest of white asparagus. He is a vegetable distributor to the local restaurants in Antwerp. To think of those fine city folk dining on my humble asparagus. I am honored!

Last week I went into town to find a replacement part for the icebox, but since the model was discontinued thirty-five years ago, I was obliged to order a whole new refrigerator, a monstrous thing with lots of confounding gadgets and gizmos.

When they took away the old icebox, I discovered a photograph that must have slipped down beneath it some years ago. It is the photograph Greta sent me of your wedding day. I have enclosed it here. If I remember correctly, next week marks your forty-fourth anniversary. What a remarkable coincidence. Bon anniversaire to my brother and friend.

Regards,
Duncan

I will give the photo to Eliza. She has begun her own photo album, in the fashion of my mother. Only she calls it a scrapbook.

She says she has been *inspired* by my mother's photography.

"Inspired to become a photographer?" I asked.

"No."

"Then what do you mean?"

"I don't know. I just feel *inspired*," she said.

CHAPTER 14

ON DECEMBER 11, 2010, I landed in Incheon International Airport, Seoul, South Korea, with three million won in my pocket, a passport that wasn't mine, and a backpack filled with nothing but spare underwear and socks.

First thing off the plane, I ducked into an airport gift shop and bought an English-Korean dictionary.

I might as well have bought a lawn gnome for all the help it turned out to be. Here is the Korean word for "Hello."

Annyeonghaseyo.

Here is the Korean word for "Thank you."

Gamsahabnida.

The language was not one I readily understood; the alphabet was not one I remotely recognized; even the way the people greeted one another, and the way they disembarked from the plane, and the way they steered through a crowd was foreign to me.

I was like a salmon swimming upstream.

I wanted to call Charlie, who had spent a few years teaching in Seoul, and whose wife was a native, to ask for advice, anything that would help me get around this foreign anthill without attracting too much attention.

But there was no way I was calling Charlie. I had told no one about my trip to South Korea or about the money or about the counterfeit passport.

I tried to imagine that conversation with Charlie: "Hey, Charlie? It's me. See, I got this gig out in South Korea, man...I've got three million won and a phony pass-port...Now all I gotta do is find a red cooler that probably contains a dead prostitute's kidney."

I decided not to mention my little Korea trip to anyone. I figured I'd be back in San Francisco before anybody caught wind that I was gone. Then I could just forget the whole thing, pretend it never happened.

The airport was huge, like being on a cruise ship bound for the Pleiades. There were spas and lounges, a private golf course, tennis courts, a casino, an ice-skating rink, and a swimming pool. Little robots roamed hither and thither, like bumblebees, doing God knows what, directing traffic or printing boarding passes or calling cabs. Talk about a vision of the future. I have never felt so utterly transported, so removed from planet Earth, so Martian, as I did when I landed at the Incheon International Airport in 2010. I half expected to look out the window and see a thousand stars suspended in the emptiness of space.

Incidentally, it was one of those little robots that told me what to do next. I was standing there like an idiot, with my mouth agape, when a blue automaton on wheels rolled up to me, looking like Rosie from *The Jetsons*. It said something in Korean, and then, after a pause, repeated in English, "How may I assist you?"

I stared at the robot for a moment. A yellow light blinked on and off, on and off, and for all I could tell, it was staring right back at me.

"How may I assist you?" it repeated.

"Lost luggage?" I said.

"Which airline?"

"Delta Air Lines."

"Terminal A," the robot said. "Follow the yellow arrows to baggage claim. Proceed down Corridor C1. Delta Air Lines will be on your left."

I have told this next part many times since, at parties and social gatherings, with my friends and family. And it almost always raises the question "Are you sure it wasn't your imagination?" I will never know. There was a lot of hustle and bustle, and the robot's voice was full of static, but this is how I remember the end of our interaction.

"Perfect," I said.

"Nothing in the universe is perfect, except maybe God, if he exists, and Oreo Cookies," the robot replied.

I have since been to Incheon International Airport two other times, and I have tried to re-create this interaction with the robot aides there, to no avail. It seems, these days, they guard the secrets of the universe more carefully.

I followed the robot's instructions and found myself standing at the main hub for Delta Air Lines in a matter of minutes. I chose the prettiest, friendliest-looking representative, a young Korean woman with a smile that took up half her face, and hoped I could use my charm to grease the wheels a bit.

"*Annyeong*," she said as I approached. "English?"

"Yes, English," I said.

"Checking in?" she asked.

"Actually, no," I said, "I seem to have lost some luggage."

"Next window, please," she said, and before I could work my magic, turn on the charm, so to speak, she yelled something in Korean, and the line shuffled forward, and I was nudged aside.

I slid down to the adjacent window, where I was greeted by a surly-looking character, much larger than my first host, and a lot less pretty.

"Uh-huh?" he grunted as he flipped through some files, which seemed to be occupying his immediate attention.

"I'd like to report some lost luggage," I said.

"Flight number?" he said, never looking up.

"Two-two-four-five," I said.

"Name?"

Here I gulped. "Logan Wallace."

He punched a few things into his computer, and then he said, "No flight two-two-four-five in the system."

"It was a few days ago," I said. "Monday, I think."

He looked up at me, eyebrows knitted. "Monday? I don't think so."

"Yes, Monday, flight two-two-four-five to Chicago. The flight was canceled, and I never received my luggage."

"You report this already?" he said.

"No, first time. First time I report this," I said.

He shook his head and let out an exaggerated sigh.

Then he disappeared into a back room.

He came back a few moments later.

"No luggage."

"Could you check again?" I pleaded. "There should be a red ice cooler."

He eyed me suspiciously for a moment.

"You have a baggage claim ticket?"

Did I have a baggage claim ticket? Oh God! Who knew those were good for anything? Of course I didn't have a baggage claim ticket. Even if I really *were* Logan Wallace, I wouldn't have kept the baggage claim ticket.

"No, I lost it," I lied.

"Then no luggage," he said and resumed thumbing through the files on his desk.

"Look," I said, "is it back there or not, the red cooler? It should have my name on it, 'Logan Wallace,' and I have my passport," at which point I laid the phony passport on his desk as means of proof.

"No ticket, no cooler," he said.

"Then it's back there?" I exclaimed. "The red cooler?"

The man picked up a newspaper and began to read.

Then, without really thinking it through, I pulled a fifty thousand won note from my pocket and laid it on the counter.

The man looked up from the paper. He frowned at the money as if it were something vile, gruesome, fecal. He looked away.

I took another ₩50,000 from my pocket and laid it on the table.

This time, the man's eyes lingered a long time on the money. Then he put the newspaper down carefully, on top of the money, rolled it up into a tube, and slipped it into his back pocket. The money was gone.

He disappeared into the back room, and when he returned, he was holding a red cooler.

"Thank you, thank you," I said, perhaps too eagerly.

He grunted and slammed the icebox down on the counter.

"Check everything is there," he said.

And then he did the unthinkable. He opened the cooler.

CHAPTER 15

THERE WERE NO LOCKS, no iron bars, no alarms to stop this man from unlatching the cooler lid and sliding it back in one swift movement, like a man firing a gun.

I was frozen, paralyzed. In a few quick seconds, this man had done the one thing I had never dared to do.

I became conscious of all the people around me: the pretty attendant chatting away at the next window, the elderly couple with the Pekingese standing at the counter beside me, the man with the impatient frown waiting his turn in line, the airport security guard pacing the adjoining corridor like a sentinel.

I imagined that their attention had turned toward me like the spotlight of a prison watch.

And because the contents of the red cooler, which were

buried deep inside the little box, were not immediately visible to me, the Delta Air Lines representative tilted the cooler forward for all the world to see.

If anyone was looking, this is what they would have seen: a turkey sandwich.

It was wrapped up in a clear plastic baggie and nestled between two melted ice packs.

The Delta Air Lines representative eyed me sternly, as if he couldn't decide whether to shake his head or laugh. *One hundred thousand won for that!* I thought. *One hundred thousand won for a turkey sandwich?*

I heard the suit behind me grunt with impatience. Surely, whatever luggage he had lost was of more value than this!

Spoiler alert: not so, not so.

Magnum Opus.

The Delta Air Lines representative clicked the lid back into place with a jerk, and pushed the icebox toward me, and then resumed reading the newspaper. I grabbed the cooler and swung around, conscious that I was holding up the line. Then something caught my eye.

A woman at the other end of the long counter slammed an identical red cooler down on the help desk. She was white, possibly European judging from her style of dress, but she spoke to the airline representative in what I assumed to be Korean. The red cooler sat between them on the counter.

The representative slipped a tag around the handle of the cooler and handed the woman a baggage claim ticket. Then the cooler disappeared behind the kiosk.

The woman turned.

She saw me and stopped dead. Her face registered something of recognition as her eyes lighted on the cooler in my hands; then, quickly, her features assumed the cold, impassive air of a sphinx.

I did nothing to hide my surprise. I just stood there, mouth agape, and considered the possibility that this woman and her red cooler had any connection to me and mine. Surely, there were other red coolers in the world, I thought.

Then the woman turned stiffly on her heel, as if pulling herself away from the scene of an accident, and disappeared into the fray. Before I could think what this strange coincidence could mean, the woman was gone.

I caught a flight home within the hour, and was sleeping in my own bed by the same time the next day. Customs had been easy. I didn't claim anything, and they didn't bother me about it. Besides, there were no laws about bringing a turkey sandwich into the country.

I e-mailed Happy Happy Happy Message Runners, Inc. as soon as I got home, and they reminded me where and when to meet the man in the Santa suit, and then the whole thing was out of my hands, and I was ten thousand tax-free dollars richer—oh, plus the five hundred thousand Korean won that Santa said I could keep.

Merry Christmas to me.

All was fine and dandy. Except my mind kept going back to the woman with the red cooler. I felt like Tarzan having encountered Jane in the jungle. For such a long time there had been only me, roaming solitary through the world, delivering red coolers. Was I alone? Were there others like me?

And then out of the mists of the jungle there had appeared this woman, a woman with a red cooler.

She stayed with me for some time, reappearing to me in dreams and hallucinations as the winter grew colder. But with Christmas parties and New Year's parties and Chanukah parties, and with visiting my parents in Malibu, and then with the blind date with a Santa Clara grad student—a redhead finishing a PhD in music theory, whom I had to commute forty-five miles each way to see—and with no subsequent contact from Happy Happy Happy Message Runners, Inc., the memory of Seoul, of the woman with the cooler, of the turkey sandwich, began to fade away.

Then in the first week of February, when my life seemed to be taking on an easy, predictable rhythm—I was still dating Jen from Santa Clara, and I was having brunch with friends on Sundays, and I was jogging in Golden Gate Park—more typical of the other twentysomethings I knew, I received another package in the mail.

In my last e-mail to Happy Happy Happy Message Runners, Inc., I had given the company my new address, thinking I didn't want them sending another counterfeit passport to the wrong guy, and knowing the post office would not keep forwarding my mail indefinitely.

My concern proved to be well-founded.

An envelope arrived with another fake passport, this time with the alias "Brooke Buchanan," and a plane ticket to Paris, and two thousand euros, for a return flight, and, guess what?

Five thousand US dollars with the promise of ten thousand more if I decided to take on a new mission.

CHAPTER 16

YESTERDAY was an exciting day here at the house. It was Pilar's day to clean, and I had promised to be out of the house, which Pilar prefers since I tend to forget when she has just mopped or waxed the floors, and she doesn't much like it when I leave footprints all over the place like a wet dog.

It was the big day of my appointment with Dr. Haug, the brain guy, and Eliza was coming over at noon to take me to get my mind downloaded to a tiny microchip. I hadn't eaten in twenty-four hours, per Dr. Haug's instructions, and had been prescribed a muscle relaxant in preparation for the procedure. I was also supposed to be exercising twenty minutes every day, Dr. Haug said, for a speedy recovery. He said the process felt a lot like whiplash; only, I wouldn't be awake for any of it. However, for a few days afterward, I'd be groggy, and my neck and spine would be sore, and there would be some temporary memory loss, but people who exercised regularly tended to experience fewer side effects.

The muscle relaxant was making me sleepy, and a little stupid, so I didn't get much writing done last week, much less any exercising.

Eliza said, "Stop wasting your time on that book of yours. We'll have your whole life story on a microchip in a few days."

I'd like to know what she thinks would be a better use of my time. All I've got is time. And money. Time and money. If you are worried about not having enough time on this planet, wait until you are pushing seventy-five, and then tell me if you still think there isn't enough time.

Eliza has a gas-powered car that she drives only on special occasions—because fuel is so expensive. She was going to chauffeur me to the clinic since she wanted to do some shopping while I was getting my brain downloaded, and the clinic is in Palo Alto, and Eliza likes the shopping out that way. The procedure takes about four hours. Eliza was going to drive me home after it was all done, get my dinner going, and put me to bed, since she said I'd be too much of a zombie to do anything myself.

So on the special day—yesterday—Eliza arrived about an hour early. I was still in bed reading the paper, like I do, and Pilar had already started on the kitchen. Eliza was early because she wanted to get into the attic. She said there were still some boxes up there from my mother's condo, and she wanted to see if she could find any more old photographs. She was working on a family tree for her scrapbook, she said, with pictures.

The attic is accessible by a steep staircase that could more aptly be called a ladder, which descends from the ceiling by pulling a cord. Eliza insisted Pilar stop in the middle of mopping to climb three flights of stairs and lower it for her.

I was still in bed when I heard the scream. Eliza had slipped scaling the staircase and had landed with a crunch on the floor. I have never heard so many obscenities out of the mouth of one person. Pilar was standing there looking dumb-founded.

"She only fell a few feet," was all she could manage to say to me.

Eliza has a habit of exaggerating. For example, when she had her first period, she told her mother that her intestines were falling out. And when she was in a minor car accident as a teenager, she claimed to have blacked out, and com-plains to this day how the car crash ruined her back. Kendra

Ann, who was in the car with her at the time, described it as a fender bender.

I doubted Eliza was in much pain. However, when we slipped off her shoe, which took a considerable effort, we saw how swollen the ankle was, and how discolored it looked, and we all agreed she had to see a doctor.

Since I am not allowed to drive, and because Eliza was indisposed, Pilar had to drive. The emergency room is just around the corner. Nevertheless, we had to sit in the waiting room an hour to be seen, and at one point I think Eliza passed out from the pain, although I still suspect it was an act. Eliza has a penchant for dramatic flair.

As it turns out, she shattered her heel bone. We were in the emergency room for six hours while they fitted her for a cast. Pilar stayed with me the whole time.

When we could finally go in to see Eliza, the first thing my darling girl said to me was: "I'm so mad at you for missing your appointment."

Eliza called this morning from bed, where her poor daughters are attending to her every need. She hasn't been able to reschedule my appointment with Dr. Haug. He's all booked up. And since I will be gone all summer in Paris with Spencer, there's no likelihood of squeezing me in anytime soon. She made sure to put special emphasis on the words "*Paris* with *Spencer*." I don't think she much approves of my going.

Dr. Haug assured her that he is looking into setting up an appointment for sometime after Christmas.

"Can you believe that?" Eliza said to me. "You could be dead by Christmas!"

Eliza doesn't much approve of my going to *Paris with Spencer*, I think, because she is afraid I won't come back. Paris is a very special place to me. It is where I met Greta. She spent her young adult life there, in and around the Sorbonne. I, too, spent a great deal of time in Paris in my youth, but never before Happy Happy Happy Message Runners, Inc. sent me there on a phony passport.

My flight was scheduled to depart on Valentine's Day. Jen and I were planning to spend the holiday in Napa Valley floating over the vineyards in a hot air balloon, munching on pâté and sipping Chardonnay. Jen's idea, my money.

She had even requested the day off from her internship at the San Francisco Conservatory of Music. Jen wanted to be a high school music teacher. She wanted to change lives. Incidentally, she went on to teach at the prestigious Vivian Strauss High School for Performing Arts in San Francisco and was named the 2022 National Teacher of the Year by the US secretary of education. After she died, the high school named a building after her, the Jennifer Abbott Library of Music, and the walls of the foyer are decorated with over two hundred testimonials from students who claim Jennifer Abbott changed their lives.

My testimonial, if I had written one, would have read, "I'm sorry, Jen, for standing you up on Valentine's Day to go to Paris. And I'm sorry that I never called you when I came back."

I flew to Paris on Valentine's Day 2011, a romantic prospect if it hadn't been for the fact that I was going illegally on a phony passport to spend less than fourteen hours there under the alias Brooke Buchanan.

Ah, Paris.

The instructions in the letter, which might have proved sufficient to any well-traveled courier with some working knowledge of French and the Parisian metro system, were to me as indecipherable as hieroglyphs.

I was to disembark at Charles de Gaulle Airport, take the RER B line to the Luxembourg station. The pickup was scheduled for 1400, which I understood to mean two o'clock, at the Jardin du Luxembourg, in front of the bust of

Édouard Branly.

I arrived in Paris at 10:00 a.m. on February 15, nearly a full day after my departure. I had taken Benadryl on the plane to help me sleep, but I had only managed to get in a few hours of shut-eye before the gal in the window seat decided to have an attack of diarrhea that required my letting her in and out of the aisle every fifteen minutes.

I was ragged and smelly when we landed, and I had roughly four hours before the pickup and nowhere to go in the meantime to nap or shower. I bought a map from the stationmaster at the Charles de Gaulle metro station, and a city day pass, and decided to make the most of my €2,000 to do a little sight-seeing.

I started at the Louvre and joined the line of anxious tourists all craning their necks to see the *Mona Lisa*, which is about the size of a dressing table mirror and impossible to see above the heads of the camera-happy lemmings. I got lost looking for Aphrodite and found myself in a half-deserted wing of the museum showcasing Dutch and Flemish painters.

The smell, the look, and the air there took me back to my high school summers working in the antique shop with my father. I even recognized the names of one or two of the painters as names that had passed through our store at some point in the hazy past.

I wound my way past Ingres and de La Tour and Van Eyck, numb to the splendor looming all around me and feeling like one submerged at the bottom of the ocean. I found myself on a bench, staring up at Van Thulden's rendering of the Resurrection and thinking what a colossal hangover Christ must have had, being awakened so suddenly from the deepest of sleeps, eternal sleep.

I was awakened in much the same fashion sometime later by a docent of the museum, explaining to me in French that there was no lying down on the benches.

It was a quarter to two. It took two trains and thirty minutes to get to Luxembourg Gardens. The park was across the street from the station, but it was bigger than I expected, so I found myself wandering around looking for the bust of Édouard Branly, whom I did not know from Adam.

I saw the red cooler before I saw the bust. And then I saw the woman. She was reclining in a green patio chair, one of the hundreds strewn about the park for sitting in and sunning in and smoking cigarettes in.

She was reading a book, and I cannot recall now precisely which book it was, except that it was a French translation of an Agatha Christie novel. The woman wore a woolen hat pulled down over her ears (it was forty degrees

Fahrenheit, and snow still lay in patches on the ground) and a long gray overcoat.

She was the woman. The woman from Seoul. The woman with the red cooler.

And here she was again, with a cooler at her side, looking like she had come for a picnic lunch.

When she saw me, she laid the book in her lap and motioned to the empty chair beside her. I took it.

"You're late," she said.

"I'm sorry."

"You know what to do with it, I suppose." She indicated the red cooler.

"Yeah," I said.

"Okay, then," and she stood up to leave.

"Hold on!" I interjected. "Didn't I see you in Seoul?"

She faced me squarely. "Yes," she said. "I think so."

"Why did they send me there to find that cooler," I asked, "if you were already there?"

"Rowan thought I was dead."

"Who is Rowan?"

She looked at me, a bit surprised, and then shook her head.

"Never mind," she said, "I have to go now. Good-bye."

She started down the dirt path that led to the entrance of

the park. I called after her.

"Is it another turkey sandwich?"

"Roast beef," she answered without looking back.

And then she was gone.

I was cold and tired and hungry, and I figured I just as well ought to head home as try to make something more out of this trip. So I caught the metro to the airport, had a McDonald's dinner while I waited for my plane, and slept like a baby all the way back to the good old US of A.

This time it was a kid who picked up the cooler. We met at a coffee shop in the Ferry Building around noon the next day. I was about as worn out as I'd ever been, and I looked a mess when I showed up with the cooler at Mike's Café wearing the same clothes I'd been wearing the day I'd left for France, my hair a rat's nest, and dark circles under my eyes.

"What is it this time?" asked the kid. He looked to be about eighteen or nineteen. And then he just popped the lid open. "What is that, roast beef or something?"

"Yeah," I said, "roast beef."

"Humph," mumbled the kid, crinkling his nose. He poked at the sandwich a bit and then took it out of its plastic wrapper and took a bite. "Still good."

"You got my money?" I said.

"What?"

"You got my money? My payment?"

"Oh yeah," said the kid. He took a fat envelope out of his backpack. It was wedged between a copy of *Molecular Cell Biology* and Wisner's *Advanced Genetics*. I'd seen both those books before.

"You go to Berkeley?" I asked.

"What's it to you?"

I had never had this much communication with one of my correspondents before, and I was feeling like trying my luck.

"I was a Berkeley grad," I said, "oh-six."

"Oh yeah?" said the kid, zipping up his backpack. "What'd you major in?"

"Business."

"Sucks for you."

"Why's that?"

"There are no jobs for business majors in this economy."

"Well, I do fine," I said, holding up the envelope of cash.

"I bet you do," the kid said. "What's Rowan paying you?"

That name again! Rowan!

But I knew better than to ask outright who Rowan was. I had seen how quickly the woman in Paris clammed up when it was apparent I knew less than she did. So I played it cool.

"What's he paying you?" I retaliated.

"He's paying for my college education; that's what he's paying," said the kid. "He's my uncle."

"What do you study?" I asked.

"Genetics and plant biology," said the kid.

"So Rowan's got a smart kid like you delivering sandwiches," I laughed.

The kid gave me a funny look, as if he wasn't sure if I was making a joke. He squinted his eyes up real tight, scrutinizing me. I could tell he was trying to make up his mind about something.

Then he said real carefully, "Yeah, he's got me delivering sandwiches."

He threw his bag over his shoulder and picked up the cooler. Then he said, pointing to the envelope of cash, "You want to make some real money, businessman? Invest some of that in InfraGen Tech."

I went online as soon as I got home and looked up Infra-Gen Tech. There was an InfraGen Technology, Inc. based out of Livermore, California. It was a tiny little start-up with hardly more than a home page and a stock ticker that resembled a dying man's EKG.

The home page read:

> InfraGen Technology, Inc. is an American-based research company that specializes in developing new technology for preserving the viability of seeds and spores for agrarian use. Founder Dr. Rowan Krasimir is a graduate of Harvard Medical School and a recipient of the Green Nation Award for his doctoral thesis, "The Extinction of Endemic Plant Species in Mesoamerica."

And that was it. No links. No contacts. Nothing more to the website than a banner and a short bio. It looked as if a third grader had designed it.

Their stock was valued at sixty-two cents a share, and had a year-to-date high of two dollars eighty-three cents and a low of thirteen cents a share. And if I could say the stock was trending in any direction in recent years, I would say the direction was down.

I already owned stocks in Apple and Amazon and Chipotle and Monster Energy Drinks, and they were doing me proud.

What the hell, I thought, weighing the envelope of cash in my hands. *What's ten thousand dollars?*

And I bought sixteen thousand shares of InfraGen Tech.

Magnum Opus.

I turned twenty-eight that month. I had always had the feeling twenty-eight would mean something great, like I would finally be all grown up and life wouldn't deal me any more surprises. I didn't know then that life never stops dealing you surprises and that the biggest surprises always happen when it looks like everything is finally settling down.

It looked like everything was finally settling down. I hadn't heard from Happy Happy Happy Message Runners, Inc. in about two weeks, which was fine by me. I wasn't anywhere near short on cash, and I'd just as soon take a little vacation from jet-setting around with phony passports.

My sister had opened a free clinic in Haiti, run by priests and nuns and staffed by young doctors just out of med school looking to volunteer for a good cause. The clinic was funded by donations pouring in from around the world, or so the press said. But I knew where the real bulk of the money was coming from.

Marilee had sold her entire collection: the American Girl dollhouse, the lawn jockeys, the giant porcelain cow she had done over with images of all the animals in the rain forests that were now endangered because their habitats were being cleared away to make room for cattle grazing, the office cubicle that was decoupaged to look like a summer day in the park.

All of it was going to a buyer from Argentina named Emilio Duarte, who planned to open a private museum in New York called the Museum of Contemporary Idiots, which was dedicated to art, like Marilee's, that drew attention to controversial global topics, like oil drilling and poaching and religious persecution.

Novocain for fools, my father would have said.

Marilee sold the collection for $1,270,000. I had to meet with the attorneys and agents at the Transamerica building to oversee the transaction, since Marilee could not be persuaded to leave her work in Haiti, even for a day.

Every cent from the sale of that collection went into the formation of a private endowment, now called the Saint Marilee Lorenzo Fund, which financed Marilee's clinic in Haiti, christened the Holy Rosary Free Clinic. The fund continues to subsidize hundreds of other clinics just like it today.

Rasima Rasima was installed as director of outpatient care at the Holy Rosary Free Clinic, a fancy title that bore no real weight, since Rasima Rasima didn't have any real medical training.

Rasima Rasima tended to the patients at Holy Rosary after the doctors administered their preliminary care, or while the patients were waiting on tests, or while they convalesced. It was her job to see to their everyday needs while they stayed in the hospital, be it for an hour, a day, or longer. She brought snacks and water, helped the patients to the restroom, gave them something to read, calmed them when they were frightened, showed them how to work the remote control, prayed with them if they happened to pray, and when finally it was time for them to check out, Rasima Rasima set to work changing the bedsheets and restocking the cabinets to make the room ready to receive the next invalid.

Although she was not authorized to directly treat patients, Rasima Rasima was well versed in homeopathic treatments, which some patients preferred, and which she administered here or there upon request. Although she had joined the convent and had renounced many of the practices and teachings of the East Indies, she still retained a vast knowledge of herbal remedies and natural therapies, which sometimes did the trick when Western medicine proved insufficient.

The Holy Rosary Free Clinic had once been a boarding school for girls. The walls of six adjoining classrooms were knocked down to clear space for the primary care center, which housed examination rooms, operating tables, and labs.

Another two classrooms were transformed into administrative offices. The girls' dormitory became a ward for convalescent and hospice care. The doctors, who were mostly young medical students from the United States, stayed in makeshift barracks north of the school yard. They had access to the old gym, which had been converted into a mess hall and recreation center. The friars and nuns were housed in what used to be the faculty quarters. This included a dozen small private apartments, a kitchen, and a modest living space. The library remained a library, and the chapel stayed a chapel.

I have visited the Holy Rosary Free Clinic only once in my life, three years ago. I was invited by the newest director of the clinic, an exuberant twentysomething, who, upon learning that the brother of Our Lady Saint Marilee Lorenzo of San Francisco was still alive and had never seen the clinic, insisted that I be flown out for a tour and to attend a special mass in honor of my late, great sister.

I accepted. I had never been to Haiti.

It is not uncommon for those who hold my sister in high regard to expect the same sort of holiness of me, her flesh and blood, as they got from Marilee when she was alive. When I am introduced to people who once knew Marilee, or who have spent their lives studying her good works, I get the impression that they are expecting a sort of Mahatma Gandhi incarnate. What they get instead is a tired, old atheist.

Nevertheless, I have always been treated with the greatest respect by those who loved my sister. When the workers at Holy Rosary saw that I did not take Communion with them at the mass, they only seemed to redouble their efforts to make me feel at home, and were kind enough to excuse me from blessing the food and leading the evening prayer, honors usually reserved for their hallowed guests.

My father was an atheist, too. He lied when he met my mother in Milan and pretended to be a Protestant, which he assumed was pretty much the same thing as a Catholic.

My mother was young, and wholly devout, and God knows a Protestant and a Catholic could never work out, she thought. But she prayed on it, and she believed, in her prayers, that God was telling her to marry this Protestant man—that a man of God is a man of God, whether he worships kneeling or standing.

What God didn't tell her was that my father was a phony.

My father kept up the charade for a while, nodding his head in prayer when my mother would say grace, or going with my mother to church on the holiest of holy days. But by and by, it became apparent to my mother that my father had never communed with God a day in his life, and that everything he owned in this world, he had come by through lying and cheating.

Even the acquisition of the antique shop in Malibu had been dubious. The property, which was ideally situated along the Pacific Coast Highway between Malibu and Pacific Palisades, and which was subject to a heavy flow of celebrities and wealthy tourists, had once been a run-down fishing and tackle store.

My father first saw the property on a trip up the coast with my mother and an old friend with known connections to the Mafia. My father had a lot of friends like that from his days in used cars and car parts. My mother claimed to have heard my father say, "It's a shame a nice property like that is going to waste selling worms." Shortly thereafter, the bank foreclosed on the property, and my father bought it for a song.

He had not yet expressed his desire to open an antique shop catering to the rich and famous, at least not to my mother.

I hesitate to add that much of what I know about my father in those early days comes from the stories my mother told me after my father had died and she had been "liberated from that ramshackle marriage." Her words, not mine.

One day my father drove out to Ontario, California, with my mother, claiming he had a surprise for her. This was about four months into the marriage, and my mother was starting to doubt my father would ever go back to work, and she was worried they were going to end up penniless and poor if he kept on gambling his money away at the race-tracks.

My father walked my mother into a mom-and-pop antique shop called Rosanne's Goodies and said, "Look around and tell me if there is anything you like."

My mother looked around. She said the place was a treasure trove of relics dating back to the nineteenth century. She asked the owner of the store where he had managed to find such fine furniture. The owner said he'd been in the business forty years, and whenever somebody in the neighborhood passed away, they sold their furniture to Rosanne's Goodies. Fine as the furniture was, the owner said, there wasn't much of a market for it in Ontario.

My mother settled on a hand-carved vanity from the 1920s, which the owner claimed once belonged to a silent film actress who retired to Ontario at the advent of talking pictures.

The story goes, and it is a famous story in our family, that my father walked up to the owner with his checkbook in hand and said, "I'll take it."

"The vanity?" the owner asked.

"Everything," said my father.

"What do you mean?" the shop owner asked.

"I'd like to buy everything in the store," my father said.

"Everything?" the shop owner gasped.

"Everything?" my mother gasped.

"Everything," my father said.

So they settled on a price—my mother never quite knew how much—and my father hired a moving company to ship all the furniture from Rosanne's Goodies out to the foreclosed fishing and tackle store in Malibu. He called the new store Pacific Antiques, a classy name that would attract a Beverly Hills clientele, and he came up with elaborate stories about all the furniture, much like the one my mother had been told about the silent film star. Then he marked everything up 30, 40, 50 percent and raked in a handsome profit.

I used to spend summers working in the antique shop. I don't remember exactly what age I was when I started, but I wasn't yet thirteen. My first job was dusting and polishing the furniture. And in junior high, I was promoted to cashier, and then in high school, I became a floor manager, and it was my job to convince potential buyers they were getting a real deal.

My sisters were never allowed to work in the shop because, my dad said, they didn't have any business sense. When it was just him and me in the store, he'd say to me, "Your sisters are as empty-headed as jellyfish. They don't know anything about the great big world out there."

Apparently I did. My father taught me how to bargain, and how to cut shady deals, like throwing in a decorative pillow with the purchase of a nineteenth-century chaise lounge, never mentioning that the pillow was on sale at IKEA for five bucks. He also showed me how to invent exciting stories for the furniture to make it more enticing.

"Fred Astaire gave this Tiffany's watch to Ginger Rogers in 1935 after filming the box office hit *Top Hat*. She wore it all her life."

We sold four watches with that story.

I thought these little fibs were fun when I was a kid. But as I got older, I started to feel more and more uncomfortable conning unsuspecting old biddies and airheaded beach bunnies and gullible tycoons into buying my father's furniture. Most of the stuff in the store would sell on its own merit; it was all very nice merchandise. But my father insisted on embellishing the truth to squeeze every nickel out of his customers.

My mother did the bookkeeping for Pacific Antiques, which was a far cry from modeling the latest fashion in Milan. And for the first ten years of her marriage, she was always either pregnant or nursing. And then she was either tying shoes or making sack lunches or picking someone up from school and taking someone to swim practice and someone to dance rehearsal and someone to tennis and someone to debate club. It wasn't until thirty years later that she finally had some room to breathe. And she looked around, and she saw that she hated her life.

Luckily for her, my father died soon after that and left her enough money to remake her life the way she wanted it.

In some ways, he was an excellent provider.

His children's children's children, namely little Marilee Junior, and Joyce and Luanne, and Rajiv and Gokul, and Tinsley and Margaret, will want for nothing.

And as far as I can tell, my father never actually "stole" a penny from anybody. I think the word I would use is "coerce." The word my mother liked to use, after my father passed away, was "con."

There is no information on my father from before Franklin Brothers Used Cars & Parts. All that is known of his past is that he grew up in Minnesota, probably somewhere near

Duluth, judging from the location of the warehouse where he kept several antique cars. His friend Rick from Minnesota came into our lives a total of two times that I can remember, the most recent of which was in 2020, when we contacted him to tell him of my father's death and to give him first pick of the antique cars.

The other time was when we went on a family vacation to Hawaii. Rick was living on Oahu, and I remember the whole family went out to dinner with him—I was eight—and Rick regaled us with stories of his travels to Thailand (I remember him saying he rode an elephant) and Egypt (he said he was hunting for lost treasure in ancient ruins, like Indiana Jones) and Peru (he explained that he owned an alpaca farm out that way). Now he was retired and learning how to surf.

My mother asked him why he wasn't married, and Rick said he had tried being married once, but it hadn't worked out because his ex-wife wanted to stay in one place, and Rick always wanted to go, go, go!

Then my mother told us it was time for bed, and she took us home, and my father stayed behind with Rick to shoot the shit.

I remember waking up the next morning and finding the hotel room filled with all sorts of curious knickknacks (I specifically remember a golden monkey from Tibet), gifts from Rick, my dad said. We shipped everything back to Malibu and marketed the collection as the exotic spoils of a notorious treasure hunter.

I think that time we were telling the truth.

CHAPTER 17

ON THE EVENING OF MARCH 10, 2011, almost a month after my last delivery for Happy Happy Happy Message Runners, Inc., I was smoking Courtney Love and flipping through the channels on my TV when news broke of a 9.0-magnitude earthquake off the coast of Japan. I was pretty baked, so I ditched Ann Curry for a *Mortal Kombat* movie instead.

When I woke up the next morning, the whole east coast of Japan had been wiped out by a thirty-foot tsunami. Thousands of people were dead or missing. Whole coastal communities had been swept out to sea. Nuclear power plants were underwater and spreading their poison far and wide.

In other words: pandemonium.

Video footage uploaded to YouTube showed a wall of water advancing inland, swallowing up cars and houses and trees and cattle and tiny screaming people. It looked like what happens to ants when you turn on the faucet in the sink.

Glub-glub!

I spent the morning glued to the TV. Every hour brought new breaking news of death and destruction.

Then my phone rang. The number was blocked.

"Jim," said the caller.

The line was crackling, and I couldn't make out the voice.

"Jim," repeated the voice, "it's Marilee."

"Marilee!" I cried. "How have you been?"

"Jim, I'm going to Japan."

"You can't be serious!"

"They need volunteers—" she began, but then there was a thud and the hiss of static, and I thought I'd lost the connection.

"Jim? You still there?" She was back. "Sorry, I dropped the phone."

"Mare, there's no way you're going to get into Japan right now," I said. "The airport is underwater."

"I'm flying out with the Red Cross tonight," she said. "It's all arranged. I want to give you the number of the church where I'm staying—so you can reach me."

I copied the number down on a Post-it and stuck it to the fridge.

"Jim," she began, and then another thud. There was a scuffle on the other end of the line, and then "Jim? Sorry, dropped the phone again."

"You're overworked."

"Nah," she said, "just distracted."

"Mare, please be careful over there."

"Tell Mom, will you?" she said. "And the others?"

"Yeah, of course." Then I thought of something. "Mare, before you go—"

"Yeah?"

"Your lawyer, that guy I dealt with when we were selling your art. He called the other day and left a message for me saying he was sending something over in the mail, something important, and that I should look it over and get back to him right away. You have any idea what he's talking about?"

There was silence on the other end of the line.

"Mare, you still there?" I asked.

"Yeah," she said. "It's probably just some legal stuff. Look, Jim, I have to go. We can talk about it later, okay? You know how to reach me! I love you gobs and oodles,

oodles and gobs."

Click.

The media followed my sister to Japan. "Local Humanitarian Joins Rescue Efforts," said the *Chronicle*. CNN aired footage of a Red Cross helicopter setting down in Tateyama and my sister climbing from the cabin to a welcoming committee of blue-haired nuns. The news crawl read, "Sister Marilee Lorenzo arrives in Tateyama. Red Cross relief efforts under way." The *New York Times* took a little more liberty: "Sister Marilee Lorenzo: Angel of Mercy."

A few days later, a large manila envelope arrived in the mail. At first I thought it was another assignment from Happy Happy Happy Message Runners, Inc., but then I noticed the return address, The Legal Offices of Oliver Sykes, my sister's attorney.

The envelope contained a twenty-page document that read like *War and Peace*.

> In the event that UNDERSIGNED should become incapacitated and unable to make decisions regarding health care, as determined by a licensed medical professional, JIM LORENZO FROST, brother of UNDERSIGNED, shall be given power of attorney, and therein

shall act as AGENT, making all decisions on behalf of UNDERSIGNED until time of death, whereupon all assets belonging to UNDERSIGNED will be liquidated and the proceeds bequeathed to said TRUST, to be overseen by aforementioned COMMITTEE.

Et cetera, et cetera.

It was a living will making provisions for Marilee's death and naming me as her guardian in the event she should become too ill to care for herself.

Why the hell would my twenty-five-year-old sister need a living will?

There was a note from Oliver Sykes, which said, "Look over the following documents and let me know if you have any questions. When you have read the documents, please initial and sign under AGENT, and return to my office ASAP."

Like hell I was going to sign anything like that. It was too morbid to even think about. Better to pretend I'd never seen it.

As my mother used to say, "Don't give the devil any ideas."

I wasn't around to take Oliver Sykes's next call, or the next, or the next. I was on a flight bound for Paris. Happy

Happy Happy Message Runners, Inc. had another job for me. I was assigned to pick up a package at the Café Père Tranquille at 16 rue Pierre Lescot, Paris, France, at eighteen hundred hours on March 15, 2011.

My flight got in at four o'clock, and it was almost five by the time I reached the train station. I took the RER B line to Les Halles, about a thirty-minute commute. The train was full of dour-faced Parisians with impassive expressions and pouty upper lips. I tried making conversation with the guy sitting across from me on the train, but he shook his head and said something in French that I understood to mean he didn't know, or perhaps didn't care to speak, English.

I had taken a couple of French lessons from iTunes since my last visit. Something about the woman in Luxembourg Gardens, something about how she spoke English so well, although she was clearly a native French speaker, something about her lingual dexterity had inspired me to try my hand at another language.

Or maybe it was just something about *her*.

I knew a few key phrases, like "Where is the fill-in-the-blank" and "Excuse me, sir" and "Sorry, madame" and "Thank you, miss" and "May I order a fill-in-the-blank, please?"

Ouais, je savais un petit quelque chose.

I'll say one thing, French was sure as hell a lot easier than Korean.

"Oú est le Café Père Tranquille," I so deftly asked a gentleman standing at the top of the stairs as I exited the metro station.

"Tout droit, sur la droite," the man said.

"Merci beaucoup," I said.

Foot traffic in Paris is about as bad as rush hour traffic in Los Angeles. I found myself weaving and swerving around old ladies and pushcarts and strollers. Once or twice I found myself in a head-on collision with an oncoming stranger.

It was "Pardon, excusez-moi, pardon, pardonnez-moi" all the way there.

The café was a corner joint with wicker chairs and *tables-pour-deux* spilling out onto the sidewalk and into the street. The ground floor was encased in floor-to-ceiling mirrors, cracked and yellowed, giving it the look of a carnival funhouse. I took a seat just inside, by a tall window facing the street, and ordered a coffee that cost something like five euros.

There was a woman sitting at the next table over stroking a black cat in her lap. The cat was purring loudly. The woman was reading a newspaper. The front page had a picture of a nuclear plant in Japan standing knee-deep in water. I couldn't read the headline, but I understood the word *Évacuation*, which was smeared all over the article like spots on a Dalmatian.

I sipped my coffee, waiting for someone with a red cooler to appear—hoping for the woman from Luxembourg Gardens to appear.

I sat there for twenty minutes, growing impatient. I ordered another coffee and then asked for directions to the bathroom.

The waiter pointed to a staircase I hadn't noticed before. I ascended the stairs and discovered a second floor, this one carpeted, and speckled with red upholstered chairs and black leather couches. The walls were lined with shelves of yellowed books, black-and-white photos of cityscapes, and large box windows affording views of the outdoor mall and gardens of Les Halles.

And there she was! The woman from the garden. This time she was in a pair of Levi's jeans and a white blouse, Tom's slip-ons, with a small onyx gem on a silver chain around her neck. A beige pea coat and matching plaid scarf were draped over her chair. She was sipping something that looked like steamed milk, which I later learned was a *vanille lait chaud*, her favorite drink, and she was reading a new book, this one in English, *The Anastasia Syndrome* by Mary

Higgins Clark.

I asked the waiter to bring my order upstairs and took a seat across from the woman. She looked up at me. Her eyes were sea green.

"Late again," she said.

"*Peut-être*," I tried.

"Not *maybe*," she countered. "Twenty minutes by my watch."

"I still have plenty of time by mine," I joked, showing her my watch, which still read 10:20 a.m. Pacific standard time.

She didn't smile, but her face relaxed a little. She stirred some sugar into her drink and took a sip.

"You found the place okay?" she said.

"Yes," I said. "It's nice."

"And your flight was pleasant?"

"I slept like a baby."

"And you fly back tonight?"

"I don't *have* to." I grinned.

Her eyes flashed. She took a few coins from her purse and slammed them on the table.

"Here is the cooler," she said, kicking it across the floor. "Good night."

"Wait!" I said as she struggled to get into her coat. "Won't you have dinner with me?"

"This is a business meeting, not a pleasure cruise, Mr. Frost," she said, trying unsuccessfully to get her right arm into her left sleeve.

She knew my name!

"You invite me to this lovely little café," I said, "I come all the way over from California, and you won't stay for dinner?"

She had squeezed into her coat, and now she was furiously wrapping her scarf around her neck, looping and looping and looping, like she was trying to hang herself.

"You got me," she spat. "I was trying to seduce you."

"Come on," I pleaded. "I just spent twelve hours on a plane. I'm starving. At least stick around to help me figure out the menu."

"Order yourself a bullshit sandwich," she said, and she was gone.

She had escaped me again. I felt a little piece of me double over. I didn't even know her name, and for all I knew, I would never see her again.

A waiter came over and asked me if I would like anything else. *What the hell,* I thought, *I'm not going to let some woman ruin Paris for me.*

I ordered the first thing on the menu, the croque-monsieur, which was just an open-face ham and cheese sandwich. It came with fries and a salad. I stuffed myself silly, and then I ordered the tarte tatin for dessert, and a Perrier to wash it down.

I asked the waiter if there was anything of interest nearby, and he pointed me in the direction of Notre Dame. It was about a twenty-minute walk. It started to rain a little, but I didn't mind, and it only lasted a few minutes before the clouds opened up to reveal the stars.

I traversed the Pont Notre Dame to the serenade of a brass band doing an upbeat rendition of "Make Someone Happy." The musicians were kids, probably no older than seventeen or eighteen, drinking wine and smoking hand-rolled cigarettes.

I found myself staring up at the grandiose towers of Notre Dame, wondering if Quasimodo was up there now, and thinking that my chances with the woman at Père Tranquille were about as good as Quasimodo's chances with the gypsy Esmeralda. And then I found myself thinking of my sister and hoping that she would someday take time off from her do-gooding, enough to visit Paris and see Notre Dame glistening in the rain, looming above the Seine. This cathe-dral, this holy place, this hallowed hall, this monument to God wasn't for an atheist like me, I thought; it was for Marilee.

I didn't have a camera, and even if I did, a picture wouldn't do the reality of the thing justice, and it certainly wouldn't bring Marilee home from Japan, I thought.

I crossed the Petit Pont to the Latin Quarter and found the nearest metro station. I rode the RER C to Champ de Mars and emerged in the shadow of the Eiffel Tower, which was ablaze with sparkling lights that came to life every hour, on the hour, like a cuckoo clock. It was like seeing Godzilla or King Kong. It was so massive, so dazzling, so imperious.

I wandered into the Parc du Champ de Mars, a long green carpet laid out at the feet of the Eiffel Tower. There were couples huddling together on blankets, and gaggles of university kids sharing bottles of wine.

I sat cross-legged in the grass, and a posse of hipsters offered me a joint and something to drink. I think it was whiskey. I accepted, and there I sat for a long time, puffing away and staring at some lucky bastard's gift to mankind.

Magnum Opus.

At about midnight it started to rain. Everyone in the park scattered, and I thought of Japan, and my sister, and everything she had done, which I had to admit, all seemed so futile to me in that moment.

I caught the last train back to the airport and managed to squeeze onto a direct flight back to California. I slept the whole way home.

When I woke up, we were circling over San Francisco. From my cabin window, I could just barely make out the towers of the Golden Gate Bridge peeking through a layer of white fog. Some other lucky bastard's gift to mankind.

Magnum Opus.

CHAPTER 18

AIR TRAVEL isn't what it used to be. Yesterday's flight to New York was nearly empty. There were maybe fifty people on a plane built for two hundred. When gas prices skyrocketed in the thirties, so did the price of a plane ticket.

Fortunately, I can afford to fly, and so can my children, and their children, thanks in part to my dear old dad. But most of today's children will never travel so far as a few hundred miles from the place of their birth, at least that's what a recent study in the *Economist* said.

And here I am in New York, two thousand miles from my house on Gough Street.

I wonder if old Eleanor Summerland, the widow of Lafayette Park, misses me.

I'm staying with Spencer and Eugene for a few weeks in

their Manhattan loft before we all depart for Paris. The girls, Tinsley and Margaret, have never been to Paris. They are big into Disney princesses right now, and they wear princess outfits around the loft: Sleeping Beauty and Snow White and Belle and Cinderella. I told them their grandmother was a princess, but she was in disguise when I first met her, so I didn't know she was a princess.

"How was she disguised?" Tinsley asked.

"As an evil witch," I said.

Greta, if you're up there somewhere, take that!

The girls can't wait to be in Paris. Tinsley thinks she's going to meet a Prince Charming over there.

"He'll be just like you, Grandpa," she said.

She is only nine.

Margaret, who, these days, prefers to go by Maggie, is more interested in trying escargot. Somebody at school told her they ate snails in France, and she said she was going to try them so she could come back to New York and say she had eaten snails and she wasn't afraid. Spencer said he worries about Maggie because she likes a dare a little too much.

"Like her grandmother," I said.

"She isn't genetically related," Spencer reminded me.

"That doesn't mean they aren't alike," I reminded him.

Spencer finishes teaching a course at NYU next week, and the girls get out of school the week after that. We're all set to fly out on June 3. I'm nervous. I haven't been to Paris since Greta died. And I've got that feeling in my stomach I used to get when I was younger, like something is about to begin. It isn't too often you feel like something is about to begin at the age of seventy-three.

I felt that way when I got back to San Francisco in 2011, after my most recent encounter with the elusive woman with the red coolers. Something was about to begin. Or had already begun.

I remember thinking, *I better work on my French.*

"Boy, are you in trouble," the kid said to me when we met at the Bi-Rite Creamery on the edge of Dolores Park.

It was the same kid from the last delivery. He was standing in line for an ice cream. I sidled up to him like we were old pals and handed him the red cooler.

"What are you talking about?" I asked.

"Rowan got a call this morning from Greta," he said, "and I don't know what she was going on about, but she sounded pretty pissed."

Greta. That was her name.

"I dunno," I said, "probably just PMSing."

The kid laughed. "Yeah. You want something?"

The kid ordered a triple scoop of salted caramel. I ordered a single scoop of olive oil and basil. It was my favorite novelty flavor at this place.

The kid took a seat on the curb and motioned for me to join him.

"What's your name?" I asked.

"Dustin," he said. "You're Jim, right?"

"Yeah. How long you been doing this?"

"Doing what?" Dustin asked with a mouth full of ice cream.

"Working for your uncle."

"About two years," he said. "He recruited me as soon as I got accepted to Berkeley. Said he knew a way I could go to college for practically free."

"So your parents don't pay anything?" I asked.

"My dad died in the Gulf War," he said. "And my mom's in a loony bin. She's got split personalities. My grandma raised me, and she died, too, last year. So Rowan's all I got."

"It's a pretty sweet gig," I said, "delivering packages while you get a full ride to college."

"So long as we don't get caught, yeah?" he said.

That made me nervous. When I'd looked inside the most recent cooler, all I'd found was a tuna melt.

"And how are you related to Greta?" I asked.

"What?" he said. "Oh, she's just one of Rowan's researchers. She's Belgian or something. I've only met her a few times. She's all right. But she was pissed as hell about something this morning. I thought you'd know since you just came from there."

I shrugged. "You been to Paris?"

"No," he said. "Rowan won't let me go. That's why he pays you the big bucks."

And then he straightened up as if a light bulb had gone off somewhere in his head.

"Speaking of which…" he said.

He pulled a fat envelope out of his backpack and handed it to me. I tucked it away in my coat breast pocket.

"I counted it," he said. "Ten grand? Hell, I'll fly to Paris for the weekend for ten grand."

"Shut up," I said. "Want me to get mugged?"

"Just saying," said the kid, "with that kind of dough, I could have gone to Stanford."

"You got into Stanford?" I asked.

"Yeah, but you can pretty much get in anywhere when your dad's a military casualty and your mom's a whack job."

"Why'd you choose Berkeley then?" I asked.

"It's got one of the best plant biology programs in the

country," he said, "and it's close to my uncle."

I'd finished my ice cream a while ago. Dustin was just cleaning out the bottom of his cup.

"I gotta get this back to the lab," he said, indicating the red cooler. "Time sensitive, you know."

"Sure," I said.

The kid laughed. "You still don't know, do you?" He jumped on his motor scooter. "Well, keep them sandwiches coming, Jim."

When I got home, I listened to the messages from Oliver Sykes, which I'd been putting off. They were all the same thing: "Jim, just checking if you got the papers," and "Jim, Oliver again, really important you call me back about the papers," and "Jim, I need to know if you're willing to sign the papers."

He was talking about Marilee's will, of course, and I wasn't particularly keen on revisiting that subject anytime soon. I turned on CNN and ordered Chinese takeout. Netflix had just sent over *Inception*, and when I had gotten my fill of Anderson Cooper, I popped the DVD into the player and lit a doobie.

I woke up on my couch sometime around three in the morning. I did the math. That would make it seven o'clock in the evening in Japan, not too late to call Marilee. I grabbed the number off the fridge and dialed international.

A man picked up on the other end.

"Hello," I said, "I'm looking for Marilee Lorenzo."

"Sister Marilee no do interview," the man snapped.

"No, no. I'm her brother. She gave me this number to call."

There was a pause.

"What your name?" he said.

"Jim Frost. Her brother."

"One moment."

I waited for about five minutes, which cost me something like ten bucks.

"Hello," came Marilee's voice finally, "Jim?"

"Hey, Marilee," I said, perhaps too cheerily. "How are you? How's Japan?"

"Oh, Jim, it's so sad. We're doing everything we can."

"Oh," I said. "Well, I'm so proud of you. So are Mom and Dad. You're all over the news over here."

"I wish the media would just leave us alone," she said curtly. "Father Sugimoto gets twenty calls a day from reporters."

"Yeah?" I said. "Well you're the big kahuna now."

"Jim, stop it," she said. "I don't do any more than the rest of the volunteers."

"I hope you're taking care of yourself," I said, "staying safe."

"Of course," she said. "We're all taking care of each other. And Sister Rosemary just flew out to help. We're opening an orphanage in a month or so, and I think another clinic."

By Sister Rosemary, she meant Rasima Rasima, who had stayed in Haiti to tie up some loose ends at the Holy Rosary Free Clinic before flying out to be with her "fearless leader," as she calls Marilee in her book.

"Marilee, I have to talk to you about something," I said. "A couple of days ago, I got something in the mail from your lawyer."

"It's late here, Jim," she said, "and tomorrow we have early morning mass."

"Marilee, this really can't wait. Your lawyer has been calling me nonstop."

There was a pause and then a long sigh.

"Yes, go on," she said.

"He wants me to sign a document agreeing to be your guardian in case you get too sick to care for yourself. An advance directive."

"Yes," she said.

"Why would he send me such a thing?"

"I asked him to."

"Why? You got radiation poisoning or something?" I said. "I just heard on CNN about nuclear waste in the water supply."

"No, no. Nothing like that."

"Then what is this about?"

"Jim," she said, "I'm sick."

As it turned out, she had been sick for some time. She had gone to see a specialist in Haiti because she was experiencing loss of feeling in her right arm, and occasional numbness in her feet. She held it together pretty well in public. But every now and then she'd drop something or stumble, and finally one of the nurses at the clinic recommended she go see a neurologist.

The neurologist was concerned. He said, best-case scenario, these were symptoms of stress or nerve damage. Worst case, possibly a brain tumor. They ran all sorts of tests over the course of several months. The prognosis wasn't good. Turned out there was an even worse case: amyotrophic lateral sclerosis, known more commonly as Lou Gehrig's disease.

The neurologist put Marilee on riluzole, which was proven to slow the progression of amyotrophic lateral sclerosis but not cure it. Otherwise, there was nothing anyone could do. He gave her five years max, if she was lucky.

Marilee told no one. She had good days, and she had bad days. Some days she had trouble pinning up her hair or tying her shoes. But most days she was fine. And she went on with her work: running the clinic, making house calls, bringing food to the poor, attending mass, leading prayer. Then one day she woke up, and she could not move her legs. She stayed in bed all day, praying to God it would pass.

It passed.

Then she called the Legal Offices of Oliver Sykes. She didn't want a media frenzy. She didn't want this to distract from her work. So she asked Sykes to draft up some legal safety nets.

Who else knew?

Only me and Rasima Rasima. I was not to tell anybody, not even our parents. Marilee said she was having more good days than bad. When that changed, she'd have to fess up.

Should I fly out there to be with her?

Absolutely not. She wasn't dying tomorrow. Some people with Lou Gehrig's disease lived for years and years after diagnosis. Stephen Hawking was still alive, and he'd been living with Lou Gehrig's disease for nearly fifty years. It didn't stop him. Marilee wasn't going to let it stop her, either. She'd be sure to keep me updated, and she'd come home to visit as soon as she got the chance.

That chance wouldn't come until five years later, when she'd been confined to a motorized wheelchair with tubes down her throat.

It was almost five o'clock in the morning when I got off the phone with Marilee. We had talked for two hours before she insisted on turning in for the night. I asked her, as we were saying our good-byes, which kind of day she was having today, good or bad?

"Every day that I get to do God's work is a good day," she said.

I don't particularly believe that anything Marilee did in her blessed life was ordained by some higher power. But it's fine if she thought that. Let her find peace in her own way. She took comfort knowing she had done good by the big man upstairs. My father took comfort in knowing he had weaseled every penny out of every dupe who came along. I take comfort knowing that when this whole monkey parade is finally over, I'll be done, finished, kaput.

Eliza takes comfort in knowing that somewhere, some-how the brains of all the people she loves are buzzing around on microchips like fireflies in a jar.

Eliza called today with what she says is exciting news. Dr. Haug knows of a doctor in Paris who is downloading brains now, too. He isn't a certified Humanity Co. specialist, but he's qualified, according to Dr. Haug, and he runs a little outfit out of rue Etienne Marcel, kind of an underground operation. Eliza says she managed to get me an appointment with the guy, Dr. Pierre Lavoie. It'll only cost me six thousand euros. No biggie.

Hah!

And that's not all. This guy, Lavoie, doesn't handle storage. So I'm supposed to ship this thing, this microchip, to Dr. Haug so he can submit it for storage at Humanity Co.

Oh boy.

Now I'm getting my brain poked at by some uncertified Frenchman with an "underground operation." That's reassuring. Maybe I should just jump out the nearest window.

I texted little Marilee Junior about it. She recently moved in with a boy, David Something-or-the-Other, and they are both working at Century Tech in Mountain View, California. I happen to have quite a holding in Century Tech, one of my better investments. Eliza is up in arms since Marilee Junior and David have only been dating six months and they're already living together. I reminded her that her mother and I had been on a total of a dozen dates before we decided to get married.

"But Mom died so young that you never found out what it really means to spend your whole life with one person," Eliza retaliated.

Ouch.

Marilee Junior has had her brain downloaded seventeen times. She has Eliza for a mother, after all. I texted to congratulate her on the new job and the new boyfriend and the new apartment, and to see if she had any advice on getting my brain downloaded.

She texted back: *It sux :(*

CHAPTER 19

IN MAY 2011 the media was going gaga for my sister yet again. She had opened an orphanage in Tateyama and a children's hospital in Minamiboso. All the newscasts showed her standing and smiling and waving like a happy, healthy twenty-six-year-old girl. The news of her illness hadn't leaked. I hadn't breathed a word. And I sensed Rasima Rasima was doing everything she could on her end to keep it on the down low. Rasima Rasima would later relate the whole cover-up in her book.

On bad days Rasima Rasima privately helped my sister wash and dress, and whenever she saw Marilee struggling with something, like holding a pen, turning a page, or opening a door, she would swoop in and take over, playing up her role as doting disciple. Rasima Rasima was often perceived as groveling and subservient, as "riding on the coattails of a great woman," one reporter wrote.

Rasima Rasima defends her actions in her book. She claims to have been in it for Marilee and for God. Those two alone.

"But wasn't she riding the coattails of a great woman?" theological scholar Thomas A. Rhett asks in *The Origins of a Saint*. "Didn't Rasima Rasima take advantage of Marilee Lorenzo's failing health to thrust herself into the limelight, repositioning herself as the archetypal apostle? And didn't she achieve her own degree of celebrity by doing so?"

Whatever Rasima Rasima's intent, the cover-up worked. Marilee did not seem to be slowing down. On the contrary. Her illness only seemed to redouble the fervor with which she attended to her duties. On Monday she was visiting the orphans in Tateyama, on Tuesday she was volunteering at a soup kitchen in Kamogawa, on Wednesday she was hosting a benefit for a local charity in Katsuyama, on Thursday she was holding a memorial for the lost fishermen of Onjuku, on Friday she was at the bedsides of patients in Minamiboso, on Saturday she was rebuilding the community center in the village of Awaamatsu, and on Sunday she was at mass praying for the sick, the poor, and the destitute of all races, religions, and creeds.

DO NOT RESUSCITATE

One incident, which made headlines in the United States, could have given her away. On a warm Sunday in late May, Marilee fell over unconscious in the pews of Saint Francis Cathedral during a memorial mass. There were over six hundred churchgoers in attendance. The entire congregation was abuzz. The paramedics were summoned, but Marilee regained consciousness before the ambulance arrived, and without so much as the blink of an eye, she ordered the pastor to go on. She refused medical care, accepting only a little water and Communion bread. She sat through the rest of the mass without further incident.

Marilee was only twenty-six. She had less than six years to live.

On May 23, 2011, two days after my sister fainted in the pews of Saint Francis Cathedral, I was summoned to Paris yet again. This time the pickup was sited at the steps of Sacré-Cœur, the hideous church overlooking Paris from Montmartre. The exchange was scheduled for 9:00 p.m., and I arrived at noon, so I checked into a hotel, took a warm shower, and changed into something more sophisticated than my usual jeans and T-shirt.

At around six I stepped out for dinner. My hotel was on the Champs-Élysées, so I joined the evening crowd strolling up and down the boulevard from the Grand Palais to the Arc de Triomphe. The sun was coasting above the horizon, and the sky was spotted with pink and orange clouds.

The Arc de Triomphe was open to visitors, so I paid eight euros to climb to the top for a look around. The rush hour traffic from a dozen avenues poured into the place Charles de Gaulle and looped around the Arc de Triomphe in a confused frenzy. How the buses and taxis and scooters and cars from all twenty districts of Paris can converge in one dizzying whirlpool of horns and brake lights without a single collision might very well be incontrovertible proof of God.

That's what I was thinking as I stood atop the Arc de Triomphe contemplating the sprawling city below. Beside me, an American family with a tripod was shooting a panorama of Paris, and I listened as they fixed their camera on various landmarks: the Eiffel Tower, Montparnasse, Les Invalides, and finally Sacré-Cœur. The white domes and steeples of the church stood high on a hill in the distance. My final destination for the evening.

I grabbed dinner at a little falafel place just off the main drag and then asked for directions to Sacré-Cœur. It was only seven o'clock, but I wanted to be early so that I could set up camp and establish a home field advantage. I wasn't going to keep Greta waiting this time.

I caught the metro to Anvers and walked a quarter mile to the base of Sacré-Cœur. A long grassy slope preceded the church, mounted by several long stairways. I chose a spot about midway up the hill where the slope plateaued. From there I had a clear view of anyone approaching from below.

I sat down on a bench. The church was closed, but there were still tourists all over the place, like ants on an anthill.

I waited.

After about an hour, a man appeared on the hill, carrying a red cooler. He climbed the steps to the plateau and took a seat two benches down from where I was sitting. I knew this had to be my guy, but I hoped I was wrong.

Where was Greta?

When the bell tower rang nine times, I gave up hope. I knew nothing about the mysterious woman with the red coolers. But I knew she wasn't the kind of gal who shows up late for a delivery. Moreover, the guy with the red cooler was starting to look antsy.

I went over.

"You my guy?" I said.

The man jumped. I had startled him.

"What's your name?" the man responded. He had a thick accent, French. He was clutching the cooler to his chest.

"Jim Frost," I said. "Who're you? Where's Greta?"

His mouth twitched nervously. I could tell he hadn't done this before.

"Greta had to work late in the labs," he said. "She sent me to give you this." He handed over the cooler.

"What labs?" I asked.

He answered as if he were on trial for murder.

"*Le Jardin des Plantes*," he said. "She works at le Jardin des Plantes."

"Okay," I said, swinging the cooler around. "You did good. Thanks."

The man looked relieved. He jumped off the bench and scrambled down the hill. I watched him until he was gone.

Le Jardin des Plantes, I thought. *That's a start.*

When I showed up at the Jardin des Plantes, a big botanical garden in the middle of Paris, the gates were locked. I walked the whole perimeter of the garden, from place Valhubert to rue Geoffroy Saint-Hilaire, searching for a breach in the fortress walls, or some sign of life.

Finding none, I wandered defeated through the crooked streets of Paris until I found myself in a small cocktail bar called Le Crocodile. It was brimming with students from the nearby universities, some of whom looked to be easily below the legal drinking age in the States.

I ordered a Desperado, which was a potent mix of mescal, grapefruit juice, and some other things I couldn't understand in French. It didn't take long before my head was spinning. I ordered another and sat watching the door. Every woman that walked in looked, for just a moment, exactly like Greta.

After about an hour, a pretty girl, maybe twenty or so, sidled up to me and asked if I was waiting for someone. She had an Australian accent.

I said no.

"Well my friends over there thought you looked lonely," she said, pointing to a table of blond Aussies who would ordinarily be just my type. But I shook my head.

"Thanks," I said, "I'm fine. You guys have fun."

I paid the bill and tipped probably twice what I should have since I hadn't quite figured out gratuity in France. Then I stumbled onto the metro and collapsed in my bed at the Hotel Champs-Élysées, not quite sure why I felt so miserable but knowing it had something to do with that goddamned woman with the red coolers.

The next morning I called the airport and booked a flight for later that afternoon. Since the cooler wasn't due back until the following morning, Pacific Standard Time, I had hoped to spend a little time sight-seeing.

And now I had a very clear idea what I wanted to see.

The Jardin des Plantes opened at 7:45 a.m. I was there by eight. I had brought a book to read, a John Grisham novel I had picked up at the airport bookstore as bait.

Agatha Christie. Mary Higgins Clark. The woman was clearly a sucker for mystery thrillers.

I walked the gardens for a while, my body tensing every time a tall brunette came into view, but it was always just another visitor like me, strolling or jogging or reading on a bench. Every so often I'd see an employee moving through the grounds, watering or weeding or checking something off a clipboard, but none of these turned out to be Greta.

Finally I tracked down one of the park rangers, a slight blonde in a khaki vest, and asked her if she knew where I could find Greta.

"She works here?" the girl asked. She had an accent that I couldn't quite place. Not American, not French.

"Yes, in the labs," I said.

"Oh," said the girl, "I don't know the botanists. Do you know if she works for the university?"

"I have no idea," I said.

"I'm sorry," said the girl. "Maybe you can ask one of the gardeners."

I got the same result when I approached a gardener. The

place was huge, with several private administration buildings, a paleontology museum, a mineralogy museum, two large greenhouses, an alpine grove, a hedge maze, and a small zoo.

Finally I just picked a bench to sit on and read for a while, hoping fate would throw me a bone.

But fate is frugal. At some point I knew I had to be going if I wanted to catch my flight. And I wanted to catch my flight. There were ten big ones waiting for me on the other side of the ocean. I had already checked out of the hotel and was carrying everything on me: one small backpack and the red cooler.

I flew back to San Francisco feeling as if I'd been robbed of something. I kept thinking, *What did I forget? What am I missing?* Then I'd remember the woman with the red coolers, and I'd think, *Oh. That.*

Not every love story has a happy ending. Sure enough, I did eventually marry Greta Van Bruggen. But we had our share of troubles. She cheated on me, for instance. And she died young, like everyone else in my life.

Eliza says I'm cursed. That's why it's a good idea for everyone around me to get their brains downloaded, she says.

I'd hardly say I'm cursed. But maybe you can say I've been the victim of bad genetics. And if that's the case, then I feel bad for Eliza and Spencer and Kendra Ann, and Marilee Junior and Luanne and Joyce, and Gokul and Rajiv. They've all got Greta's genetics, and mine. Heart disease, amyotrophic lateral sclerosis, cancer. In that way, I guess it's sort of like a curse. A family curse.

Lucky for Tinsley and Margaret, they're adopted.

I ought to mention that Spencer, Eugene, and I arrived in Paris Saturday. The girls are bouncing off the walls. We've been put up in this handsome little three-bedroom flat in the Marais, overlooking the Place des Vosges, the city's oldest public square.

The onetime home of Victor Hugo, now a museum, shares a wall with our flat, and throughout the day, we can hear the muffled echoes of tourists clambering about on the other side of the wall like specters in a tomb.

Today I have the flat all to myself. Spencer is at the university sorting out some paperwork, and Eugene took the girls out for ice cream. They asked if I wanted to come, but the flight over here wiped me out, and I said I'd prefer to sit by my window and watch the people come and go in the square below, and listen to the ghosts bang around next door, and perhaps get some writing done.

I got an e-mail yesterday from Sam Getz, who has read some of my book and says it needs work. *It needs to be more accessible,* he says. *Not so cerebral.*

"Get out of your head, Jim," he says in his e-mail. "Tell the story from start to finish. Stop beating around the bush. We're not interested in your children and your grand-children. We want to know about YOU."

Typical.

If I told the story from start to finish, then I guess you'd know by now that I was a pretty good beatboxer back in my day. I was goofing around with my friends in the dorms my first year at Berkeley, and one of them had a camera phone, and they took a video of me throwing down a beat while my friend Charlie rapped the Gettysburg Address. It got something like four million views on YouTube before the end of spring term.

I just checked, and it has three hundred million views now. There are too many people in the world with too much time on their hands.

I guess if I had told the story from start to finish, you'd also know by now that I lost my virginity in the ninth grade to a girl named Sally Cunningham, who was in the eleventh grade. She took advantage of me the night of the winter formal. She was tall and had big breasts. I was growing.

I have also never used a condom.

How's that for knowing about me?

When I returned from Paris in May 2011, I considered asking Dustin, the kid on the motorbike, to tell me more about Greta. But when I showed up in front of the Castro Theatre in San Francisco, the next designated meeting place, it wasn't Dustin who greeted me but a disheveled fellow in his late forties wearing Birkenstocks and a lab coat. He seemed hurried, so I didn't have time to question him. He just handed me the money and grabbed the cooler and left. But I did have a chance to get a look at the ID badge he wore clipped to his breast pocket.

Rowan Krasimir, the nametag read, *CEO InfraGen Tech.*

When I got home, I tried calling Marilee. I hadn't spoken to her since March, and I wanted to make sure she was holding up okay. I figured if she was getting worse, she wasn't about to tell me. And I was starting to get anxious about not telling our parents. I felt like the family deserved to know. After all, none of us had seen Marilee since she left for Haiti in 2010.

It was probably about 8:00 a.m. Japan time when I called.

The phone rang and rang. After about ten rings, I hung up and tried again.

This time a woman answered. She greeted me in Japanese.

"Hello," I said. "May I speak to Marilee?"

More Japanese.

"Marilee," I said. "Marilee Lorenzo."

"Ah! Mawagi Wawanso!" the woman said. "No, no."

"She's not there?" I asked.

"No, no," she repeated.

"Can you tell her Jim called?"

"No, no."

"Okay," I sighed. "Thanks anyway."

"Okay!" she said. "Bai-bai!"

Click.

CHAPTER 20

I ASKED MARILEE one time what she thought heaven was.

"It's anything you want it to be," she said.

In that case I wouldn't mind so much if heaven was a deep void of nothingness where no part of anything is distinguishable from anything else. Or a coma. A coma would be perfect.

"People wake up from comas," Spencer said to me when I shared this sentiment with him the other day. "I wouldn't ever want to wake up."

Now you're talking!

"How about a black hole?" Eugene said from the other room where he was typity-typing away at his computer.

Eugene is writing a story about a band of renegade

misfits who sail the galaxy in their spaceship, the *Jolly Roger*, and steal planets from alien solar systems. They use a special device called "the Cannon" to shrink the planets down to pocket-size, and they hold them for ransom, or trade them for gold and liquor and women, or sell them to wealthy warlords on other planets.

The captain of the *Jolly Roger* is a fellow who was badly burned in an atomic blast on his home planet, Earth. Extensive surgeries have rendered him half man and half robot.

Whenever any of the bandits violates the Pirates' Code, which is the governing law on the *Jolly Roger*, the captain makes the perpetrator walk the plank, which means he has to venture out into deep space for three minutes without a space suit. If the bandit survives, he is welcomed back onto the ship but forced to do hard labor in the galleys. If he dies, they say his soul is swallowed by a black hole.

Eugene asked me the other day if I had ever met anyone who had survived an atomic blast, like the captain of the *Jolly Roger*.

There have been only three deadly atomic blasts in the history of Earth. I cannot speak to the total number of deadly atomic blasts in the history of the universe. The three earthbound atomic blasts were Hiroshima, Nagasaki, and Atlanta, Georgia.

I met a man when I was visiting the children's hospital in Japan where my sister worked whose face had been melted off in Nagasaki. The man was working at the children's hospital as a nurse's aide. I asked my sister if the man frightened the children at all. She said sometimes, because he looked like Lord Voldemort. But mostly they just wanted to know if he knew Harry Potter.

I asked Eugene if Paris has been good for his writing. He said, as good as anywhere. He asked me the same question. I said I just hoped the ghost of Victor Hugo wasn't looking over my shoulder.

Eugene writes everything down by hand, and then when he's got about ten or fifteen pages fleshed out, he types it all up on his computer. This way, he says, he can't second-guess himself too much.

"The delete button is an easy out," he says. "I like to write forward, and if I get into a sticky spot, it's up to my characters to dig their way out."

Maybe I'd feel the same way, except I already know exactly what all my characters are going to do next.

For example, I know that Greta says yes when her old boss and lover Gerard Boule calls her up out of the blue and asks her if she's interested in going to Korea for an exciting research opportunity.

"South Korea?" Greta asks.

"Not quite," Boule says.

Greta finished her studies at Pierre and Marie Curie University in 2006, the same year I graduated with my BS in business administration. Greta was only twenty years old, and she had already completed the equivalent of an under-graduate degree in cellular and plant biology and a master's degree in biodiversity and genetics.

She had a low-wage position as a research assistant in a genetics lab associated with the Jardin des Plantes, where she had spent the last five years under Dr. Julie DuPont, a woman famous for crossbreeding a grape with a watermelon and making the world's first grapemelon, a common house-hold snack today for those who can afford it.

Greta Van Bruggen, as DuPont's assistant, was respon-sible for mapping the genetic codes of all the outlandish plant species Dr. Julie DuPont cooked up in the lab. They would cross an avocado with a guava, or a kiwi with a lemon, or a beet with a radish with a cactus, and see what turned up. Ninety-nine percent of their experiments were complete failures. Of the 1 percent that succeeded, about 99 percent of those were total abominations of nature. Imagine

Aphrodite's bust topped with the head of a scorpion. That sort of thing, but with fruit.

The remaining fraction of the successes, however, made the big time: the grapemelon, which tasted like a bite-sized splash of Kool-Aid; a strain of banana that could grow in the desert; and a variety of wheat that was gluten-free, whatever that means.

There wasn't always a demand for these freaks of nature, so if they didn't die on the vine, they very often died in the marketplace. People are very picky about their fruit. If it doesn't look like something Eve might have plucked from a tree in Eden, then usually nobody wants it, even if it costs half as much to produce, uses a fraction of the natural resources to grow, and retains ten times the nutrient content.

God didn't create the grapemelon, some religious activists will say. He didn't create the poodle either. Or the common house cat. Where did they come from? From thousands of years of meddling, that's where.

Some of the other researchers at the laboratory had a nickname for Dr. Julie DuPont. They called her Dr. Frankenstein. They had a nickname for Greta, too. They called her Igor.

Frankenstein and Igor made a fabulous team. Dr. Julie DuPont was a wide-eyed dynamo in her forties. She had been married three times and divorced just as many. She had two young children, a boy and girl, from her second marriage, and she toted them around in a canopied rickshaw on the back of her bike, since she didn't believe in the use of fossil fuels.

DuPont always had a dozen projects going at once, and she divided her time between the genetics laboratory, the classroom where she taught an advanced course on genetic sequencing, the laboratory at the Jardin des Plantes, and her children. DuPont never slept except for two or three hours in the wee small hours of the morning when the rest of the world had gone so still she couldn't get much else done, and as far as Greta knew, she survived off a strict diet of trail mix and quinoa.

Greta Van Bruggen came into DuPont's life right about the time the grapemelon made its first big splash in the scientific community and funding started pouring in from all over the country. In a matter of months, the harebrained postdoctoral scholar everyone called Frankenstein became the most respected plant geneticist in Western Europe.

Greta acted as chief of staff to DuPont, keeping her schedule, reminding her of publication deadlines, making sure she ate, not to mention single-handedly running the labs at the university and the Jardin des Plantes.

So when Greta graduated, DuPont was desperate to keep her on staff. DuPont wrangled together some funding for Greta to do independent research at the Jardin des Plantes. That would keep Greta in close enough proximity to keep things running smoothly. It guaranteed Greta a paycheck for at least another couple years, and Greta got to run her own lab, working on the projects that mattered most to her.

What mattered most to Greta Van Bruggen?

Conservation of the species, for one. It was all well and good to play God and design totally new plants, like the grapemelon. But what of the plants God had designed with his own two hands? Greta was concerned. Rising sea levels and changing weather patterns were decimating the natural environments of many rare plant species that had nowhere else to call home—she had borne witness to as much in her work with Dr. Gerard Boule in Indonesia. Moreover, large corporations were encouraging farmers to plant monocrops and GMOs—most farmers today wouldn't be able to identify the type of corn served at the first Thanksgiving dinner on Plymouth Rock. Not to mention the clearing of the rain forests, oil spills, melting ice caps, and every other manner of horror the hippie liberals were shoving down our throats in those days.

Greta wasn't a hippie liberal, per se. She liked to think of herself as a custodian. "Go ahead and do what you want with the planet," she used to say, "but you better have a damn good custodian you can call when you make a mess of it."

Greta carved out a little niche for herself isolating endangered strains of plant species, which in and of itself justified the funding, but also lent itself marvelously to DuPont's mad science. She put out a few academic papers a year, enough to appease the funding gods, and spent the rest of her time cataloguing genomes, making recommendations to the Jardin des Plantes, and helping DuPont engineer the world's first bananaberry.

Then, in 2008, she got a call from her old friend Dr. Gerard Boule. He had the perfect job for a young scientist looking to save the world.

"Okay, why not?" she said.

CHAPTER 21

LAST NIGHT I SNUCK OUT to see the opera at the Bastille. It was the premiere of Adama Busceppi's tragic tale *Il Vecchio e La Commessa*. The curtain opens on an old man on his deathbed. His nurse asks if there is anyone she can call.

"No," he says, "there is no one."

The nurse laments, "But signor, you are a good man who has devoted his life to serving God and the people. Your charity and kindness are hailed throughout the land. Good sir, you are admired by all."

"And loved by no one," he replies.

This is a rough translation. The opera was in Italian, of course.

The nurse attempts to make the old man more comfortable, but he insists, "There is nothing to do now but wait. I will sleep like the pharaohs in a few short hours."

The nurse contents herself to sit at the old man's bedside and read aloud to him from the complete works of the Archpoet, and presently she falls asleep. The old man is left staring at the ceiling, contemplating heaven. This aria, sung in an airy falsetto, makes a play on the Italian word *cielo*, which can mean both sky and heaven.

The aria comes to a gentle close, and a single flickering candle on the old man's nightstand burns out. But soon a light appears from offstage, and an angel descends from the wings.

She addresses the old man: "Good signor, you have spent your whole life in the service of God and the people. For this you are to be rewarded."

The angel tells the old man she will grant him three more days of life.

The old man protests, "Oh, good angel, do not waste three days of breath on an old man like me."

The angel laughs, "Good signor, I also grant you youth!"

Here the old man is lifted from his bed as if by an invisible hand. The bedcovers sweep over him like great waves in an ocean, and when the tumult settles, the old man has become a young, spry lad with rosy cheeks and a fine head of thick auburn hair.

"Hark, the sun rises," the angel says, indicating the brightening sky. "Go and live!"

The man, full of youth and vigor, thanks the angel and grabs his coat and rushes out the door. The angel exits.

The nurse wakes to find the bed empty and the old man missing.

"Mio Dio!" she cries. "Where has the old fool gone?" She rushes out to look for him.

The next scene finds the man on a busy city street, joyfully extolling the virtues of youth, which, he says, are wasted on the young. He helps an old innkeeper lift a wine barrel; he joins in a children's game of pitch-and-toss; he leaps over a puddle of mud and ducks under two men carrying a wooden beam; he belts out a cantata in full voice from atop a soapbox, and all the villagers applaud.

"To breathe a full breath of air and hear no rattle, to gaze upon the distant stars and see no spots, to take a step and never falter, to dance and never touch the ground—that is what it is to be young, my friends! Cherish it," he sings to a passing line of schoolchildren.

The nurse enters stage left, asking bystanders if they have seen an old man in poor health who has wandered out alone. He is sickly, with white hair and a crooked back, she says, and he can't have gone very far. The man sees the nurse, and knowing she will never recognize him in his transformed state, offers, in a bit of jest, to help her look for the missing man.

"Is he tall?" he asks the nurse.

"He was once very tall, like you are, signor," she says, "but now he is shrunken like a gnome."

"Is he handsome?" he asks.

"So far as a gnome can be handsome," she says.

"Does he have all his teeth?" he asks.

"Only when he puts them in," she says, "but he has left them on the nightstand. Mio Dio, how can I have let him out all alone, and without his teeth!"

Together they search for the old man, but finding no evidence of him anywhere, the nurse rushes offstage to look for him in another avenue.

The man is amused.

"Dear woman," he says. "Look how she worries herself sick over me. She plays a hopeless game of hide-and-seek."

But then he repents.

"I must go and apologize for playing such a wicked hoax. Flowers will do the trick."

He ducks into the flower shop.

He is greeted by a beautiful young shopgirl with whom

he falls madly in love. The rest of the opera proceeds like *Cyrano de Bergerac*. The old man, disguised as a handsome young buck, pursues the shopgirl. The shopgirl falls for the handsome young buck, unaware of his true identity.

The audience, privy to the full story, waits expectantly for the shit to hit the fan.

The romance progresses rapidly into the second day, and the man wrestles inwardly with the knowledge that he is not what his love thinks he is, and in three days' time, all will be revealed.

The whole mess is brought to a head on the third day when the nurse recognizes the old man's coat on the rosy-cheeked lad. She confronts him in private, and he confesses to everything. The nurse, sympathetic, advises him to face the shopgirl and tell the truth.

"To play a young man's game," she cautions, "is to suffer a young man's heartache."

The man thanks the nurse for her prudent advice and goes at once to tell the shopgirl the truth. They meet in the woods. It is the eve of the third day. The shopgirl is full of fanciful chatter, but the man stops her short and explains that she must quit him now, that he is a rascal and a liar.

"I am an old man and will not live through the night," he says.

"Absurd," she says. "Look at you! You are the picture of health."

"It is a mirage that will fade with the coming light," he says. "I am young for but a few hours more. Then dawn will reveal the misshapen old fool that I am."

The shopgirl is insulted and offended, and we are led to suppose it is because she has been grievously misled. But she surprises us when she reveals the true nature of her distress.

"You would brush me off so easily!" she cries. "You think me so vain as to flee at the first sign of trouble. Love is a ship you command on the high sea, through thick and thin. I will not leap overboard at the first whisper of an ill wind. I will go down with my ship. Come now, do not cast me off. Let us make the most of the time we have left."

The man is overjoyed, and they embrace as the lights fade to black. The final scene finds the man returned to his original state, much like the one I find myself in now, gray and weathered and bent. He is locked in an embrace with the young shopgirl as the sun rises over the woods. She sleeps undisturbed.

The old man sings a Latin refrain from the Archpoet's masterpiece, "His Confessions." Then the angel descends from the ceiling and takes the old man away to who knows where.

The shopgirl wakes and wonders if she has dreamed the whole affair, and then wonders if anything on this earth is any more lasting than a dream.

"The dream appears one moment, vivid and bright. We are fooled into thinking it will last forever. And then it is gone in a puff of smoke, and the angels on high laugh at our mortal folly."

There is the fury of trumpets and bass drums, and the curtain falls.

Something to think about.

I felt much the same way when Greta died. The doctor came into the waiting room. Little Eliza was asleep in my lap. Spencer was playing with a toy truck on the floor, and Kendra Ann was curled up beside him.

"Poof," the doctor said. "She's gone."

We didn't even suspect anything was wrong until it was much too late. Greta was never one to make a fuss, and when she started vomiting, we initially suspected she was pregnant again. But when several pregnancy tests and a sonogram revealed she was no more pregnant than I was, we started to worry. We got her in to see Dr. Mitzner right away. He was an eighty-two-year-old Holocaust survivor with whom Greta had some previous relationship of which I was always unclear, but I think they knew each other from Antwerp. I should really write Duncan to find out.

Dr. Mitzner had a small family practice out in Palo Alto, and Greta swore by him, so we drove all the way out there anytime one of the kids was sick or if Greta and I needed a checkup. This trip was different, though.

Greta went in to see Dr. Mitzner alone. About thirty minutes later, she came out and said we had an appointment that afternoon with a specialist, Dr. Cara Johnson over at Stanford University, in oncology.

Oncology! I remember that being one of those punch-in-the-stomach moments when you feel like the wind has been knocked out of you and you don't think you'll ever be able to breathe again.

We hadn't held hands in a long time—we were still going through the aftermath of the affair. We held hands all the way to the Stanford Medical Center and didn't let go until a nurse pulled Greta into a CT scan.

The cancer had already metastasized. Dr. Johnson wanted to keep Greta overnight to run some more tests. I went home to feed the kids. Eliza was ten, and she was furious with me because I had left them with the babysitter for much longer than I had promised, and Eliza hated it when things didn't run on schedule. That hasn't changed much.

Spencer was seven, and Kendra Ann had just turned six. They asked where their mother was, and I told them she wasn't feeling well, and she was sleeping at the hospital so she could get better faster. It was the only thing I could think of to say.

She never did get better.

She died six months later. Little Eliza was devastated. We had a rough time of it, Eliza and I. She blamed me for some things; I never quite knew what. She was only ten years old, after all, and I'm not sure she knew what she blamed me for, either.

I blamed myself for some things, too. I thought of every time in the last five years Greta had said something in passing about her stomach hurting or about how she didn't have an appetite.

"It's probably just gas," was my go-to explanation for everything.

I even thought of things from a decade before, when there couldn't have been a single cancerous cell in her body: how beer made her violently ill, how she itched whenever she ate carrots, and how she fainted for no apparent reason in the bathroom of the Beverly Hilton when we were down south for my father's funeral.

I also thought about Greta's father, who had died at the age of forty-six, they said from an enlarged heart. Somehow that seemed like a warning sign, too.

Dr. Johnson said it was most likely because Greta smoked. And no one could argue that—Greta smoked. At least a pack a day. But never in the house and never in front of the kids. In fact, the kids say they don't remember ever seeing their mother with a cigarette.

Greta was good at hiding things. That's how the kids never found out she smoked. That's how she could manage to sneak around North Korea without getting caught. That's how she could have an affair right under my nose, with Norman McCredie, the real estate agent who sold us the house on Gough Street.

The affair started some years after we had bought the house on Gough Street. In couples therapy Greta admitted that she had felt a spark for Norman the Real Estate Agent the moment she met him back in 2019, when we were look-ing to upgrade from the house on Ortega to something more roomy. But at the time, Greta didn't have the energy to get involved in a messy affair. Kendra Ann was still breastfeed-ing, and Eliza had just started preschool.

But then sometime in 2022, I don't know precisely when, Greta ran into Norman McCredie at an art auction. She went to art auctions all the time, even though she never bid on anything. She bought the Degas at an art auction. And two Gerhard Richters. That was it. She bought those sometime in 2022, maybe the same time she ran into Norman McCredie. I don't know. The therapist said it was best if we didn't hash out the minor details of the affair.

I can't ask Greta now about the minor details of the affair. And I can't ask Norman McCredie, either. He is dead, too. A skiing accident in 2037. Serves him right.

I guess when they bumped into each other at the art auction in 2022, Norman McCredie mentioned something about trouble with the missus at home. The therapist said that was a common pickup line among serial adulterers, saying there was trouble at home. If that's the case, then Greta took the bait, hook, line, and sinker.

She and I weren't exactly Mr. and Mrs. Happily-Ever-After, either. I had become a bit of a do-nothing ever since we had come into my father's money. I took a few jobs for Happy Happy Happy Message Runners, Inc., which I knew by then to be a cover for InfraGen Tech's illicit dealings. And I spent the rest of my time at home smoking pot and making bad investments in high-tech start-ups that eventually went bust. Thank goodness for the few that didn't. They more than made up for the difference. But not right away, and not in 2022.

Greta had taken a "real" job as a researcher for InfraGen Tech in Livermore, about a forty-minute commute from the city. She was still interested in saving the world. And she was single-handedly raising the kids. I conceded as much in therapy. Obviously all that changed when she died and left me a single dad.

When Norman McCredie waltzed into her life complaining of troubles at home, of course Greta was seduced. Here was a man who understood what she was going through.

I would bet anything he had used that line before: *troubles at home*. He'd had at least one other affair before. He told Greta as much. The therapist said that telling her about his previous affair was his way of planting the idea in her head and seeing how it would take.

It took.

The affair went on for about a year. I was completely oblivious. I didn't know she was lying about having to work late. For as long as I'd known her, she'd had to work late. They carried the whole thing out in the recently vacated condos of unsuspecting homeowners who had given Norman McCredie their business—and their front door keys.

This was a common practice in the real estate world, said the marriage counselor. She knew of a dozen other such cases.

Greta stopped seeing Norman the Real Estate Agent around Christmas of 2022. A New Year's resolution, she said in therapy. I'd have never found out. But six months later, Norman called me up out of the blue and confessed to the whole thing.

Why? He had become a born-again Christian and wanted to ask my forgiveness, presumably because he wanted to improve his chances of getting into heaven.

If this were Eugene's story, and I were the badly burned captain of the *Jolly Roger*, you know what I'd have given Norman McCredie? Three minutes in deep space without a space suit.

It took less than twenty seconds for Norman to explain what had happened. He wanted to go on, to *elaborate*.

I didn't give him the chance. I said, "Thank you very much. Now go fuck yourself," and hung up.

Let the record show, those were somebody's last words to Norman McCredie: "Go fuck yourself." Surely that will mean a whole lot of extra paperwork at border control in heaven.

Greta was repentant. She didn't make excuses or try to turn it around on me, as she could have. For the kids' sake, we stuck it out under the same roof and tried to sort through our feelings the best we could in the few quiet moments we had to ourselves. But the rest of the world kept spinning, and we were like rats on a treadmill trying to keep up with the manic pace we had set for ourselves: dance recitals, karate lessons, baseball games, family vacations, renovating, redecorating, dinner parties. Not to mention my substantial investments in the high-tech industry and Greta's ongoing research at InfraGen Tech. We were bogged down in that time of life Dr. Laura Sully, our marriage counselor, dubbed "yuppie adolescence."

We found Dr. Laura Sully entirely by accident. She was one of the other prominent donors seated at our table during a fund-raiser dinner for CALS—Cure Amyotrophic Lateral Sclerosis. She had a father who had died, like Marilee had, of Lou Gehrig's disease in 2017, and she said Marilee had been a great inspiration to her family.

We asked what Dr. Laura Sully did for a living.

"Marriage counseling," she said and handed us her card.

Sometimes it's that simple.

A few months after Dr. Sully came into our lives and just before Greta was diagnosed with cancer, things started looking up. We were talking again. Our sex life had improved. I was getting to know our children. The stock market rallied. And Greta was awarded the Xiao Ho-Chin Award for a paper she had published on genetic sequencing and evolution.

Dr. Sully gave us what she called the "Gold Star of Progress."

Then Dr. Johnson gave Greta six months to live.

It was just like *Il Vecchio e La Commessa*. Here I was in love with a ticking time bomb.

Then poof, she was gone.

I kept seeing Dr. Laura Sully after Greta died. From marriage counselor to grief counselor. Then our relationship took a romantic turn. And that took my mind off things for a while. But I couldn't shake the feeling Greta was in the room whenever we made love. As a matter of fact, I couldn't shake the feeling that Greta was everywhere I went, watching everything I did.

You see, for as long as I'd known Greta, I'd thought we shared the same idea of death. When you're gone, you're gone. Finished. Kaput. She never really talked about God. She'd say from time to time, "If God could see what we've done to this place..." talking, of course, about the planet and how we'd trashed it like a couple of teenagers whose parents were out of town. But in all our conversations, God was always mysteriously absent, away on business or some other such thing. "If God knew what a mess we've made of things," she'd say.

I always figured the rest was implied: "But he doesn't know, and he can't see, because he doesn't exist."

Then one day, shortly after she was diagnosed with cancer, we were waiting in the doctor's office for yet another disheartening report from the latest round of tests, and Greta said, because I must have looked scared: "I'll still be around, you know."

I blinked.

"I'll be hanging out with my mom and dad, and your sister, too, and we'll keep an eye out for you and the kids."

"That's very nice," I said, "but wouldn't you rather just be done with it all? I don't want to think of you rattling around in the walls like a ghost, spying on me."

She laughed. "I won't be *rattling around*, Jim. I'll be hanging out with all our friends. Everyone we've known who has died. It'll be nice."

"Do you really believe that?" I asked.

"Of course I do," she said.

"Since when?" I protested. And why hadn't she ever mentioned it to me before?

"I don't know," she said. "I guess since we had the kids."

So she had concocted this fantasy in order to counter the ever-present fear of losing her children. And now she was dying, and the fantasy worked in reverse. The children didn't have to worry about losing her. She'd always be there, partying it up with Grandpa Frost and Auntie Marilee and Gregor, who was the Labrador of ours that was run over by a truck, and Dr. Chow, the stray cat that hung around the house begging for milk until one day he didn't come around anymore, and all the dozens of goldfish we had killed. They'd all be up there together having a good time. And the kids could talk to her anytime they wanted.

Eliza latched on to the theory like it was a life raft on the sinking *Titanic*. Spencer didn't buy it. He's a lot like me. There's more comfort in knowing a person is gone for good. Why drag this whole monkey parade out any longer than it has to be? Kendra Ann recently told me she still talks to her mother every day.

So what if heaven really is whatever you want it to be, like Marilee used to say? Then perhaps I will get my way after all and disappear into the void of nothingness. But how, then, does Greta get her way, too? How can I be both gone for good *and* schmoozing with old friends at a big garden party in the sky? What then of my soul? To be or not to be? A conundrum.

DO NOT RESUSCITATE

I think my mother is also expecting a visit from me when my time is up down here on Earth.

Sounds like I have one hell of an itinerary in the afterlife.

CHAPTER 22

POOR ELIZA. She had already been to three funerals by the time she was eleven: her mother's, my sister's, and my father's. Of the three, she says she remembers Marilee's best. How could anyone forget it? The *SF Chronicle* called it an "Ecclesiastical Woodstock." Thousands of people showed up from all over the world to pay their respects. The service was restricted to a private guest list of 1,842 intimates, of which I knew maybe a dozen. Then there were hundreds of mourners who just showed up and held their own impromptu services in the streets and parks surrounding the church. The service was also broadcast live on Fox News and streamed in several large cinema complexes around the world.

I had almost no say in the planning of it. The Catholic Church appointed a committee to organize the whole affair.

My only role was to nod yes or no when a representative of the committee approached me with details regarding the wishes of the immediate family.

The service was held in the Grace Cathedral on Nob Hill in San Francisco. Helicopter footage of that day shows crowds of mourners clogging the streets and thoroughfares for ten blocks in every direction.

The mayor of San Francisco spoke, as did the Archbishop Thurgood M. Dryden, and Rasima Rasima, and several celebrities, including Norma Watts, who had recently portrayed Marilee in a made-for-TV movie about the earthquake in Haiti. I spoke, but I can't for the life of me remember what I said. I certainly couldn't have said what I was thinking: may she be forever gone, dead, finished, kaput. My sisters couldn't muster the nerve to address the congregation, but my mother spoke, and she said some very nice things that made sense to the contingency of bible-thumpers.

My father did not attend. He and Marilee had not spoken for nearly a decade, not since he had disowned her for making Novocain for fools. And now he said he wasn't going to go to any funeral that invited half the world to come and gawk at a girl who spent her whole life wiping other people's asses.

He was a real class act, my dad.

My mother told the press that our father could not make the trip to San Francisco due to heart troubles. She didn't feel like she was lying to anybody, she told me confidentially, because our father did have heart troubles; the trouble was he had no heart.

The funeral dragged on for five hours, and then the cathedral was opened to visitors wishing to pay their respects to the inanimate remains of my sister. About twelve thousand people passed through the church in the span of six days. The church took donations, and I think something like $2 million poured in, most of which was funneled into the Sister Marilee Lorenzo Fund, now called the Saint Marilee Lorenzo Fund, and which is responsible for opening something like one hundred clinics worldwide and over two dozen orphanages, among other things.

You'd think that would be enough to get you sainted, right? Not so, not so. As I later learned, the road to sainthood is no cakewalk. First of all, the person in consideration has to be dead. Marilee had at least that much going for her. And then said person has to perform no less than two bona fide miracles while remaining dead.

"That's where Rasima Rasima comes in," wrote theological scholar Thomas A. Rhett. "There was no way Marilee Lorenzo could have fast-tracked her way to canonization from the grave. She needed an inside man."

Marilee was interred at Mission Dolores Church on Sixteenth and Dolores. The dust had barely settled on her tomb when Rasima Rasima showed up in Rome requesting an audience with the Pope. She wanted the Vatican to start right away on its consideration of Marilee Lorenzo for the distinction of sainthood.

Traditionally such a process could not commence until at least five years had passed and the lasting impacts of the candidate on the mortal world were more readily understood. But such conventions had been waived before, Rasima Rasima pointed out, when the candidate was of particular renown.

The Vatican was unmoved.

But Rasima Rasima was not deterred. She took up residence in Rome, within a few blocks of Vatican City, and spent her days campaigning for my sister. There were others, too, who joined the cause, many of them women who had worked closely with Marilee in Haiti or Japan. They were called the Nuns of Borgo Vittorio, because of the little cloister they kept on the avenue Borgo Vittorio. Every day they wrote letters, held vigils, organized prayers, all in the name of Sister Marilee Lorenzo.

Three years later the Pope consented. His decision made

headlines in the United States: "Sister Marilee Lorenzo to be Considered for Sainthood Only Three Years after Tragic Death." Imagine having a sister recently laid to rest whose name suddenly pops up again on every news crawl, blogger site, Twitter post, and Facebook thread from here to Timbuktu. There *is* such a thing as ghosts.

The Vatican assigned Bishop Carlo Devicchio to the case. He spent two years studying every detail of Marilee's life, from her childhood to her art to her charity work to her relationship with God and the church, even to her disease. When the investigation finally came round to me, I declined an interview but issued a written statement to the bishop stating that I wished to be exempt from the inquiry as I did not share the same beliefs as my sister. I did, however, add a postscript in which I expressed my deepest respect and admiration for my sister's unwavering devotion to whatever cockamamie improbability it was that resulted in the universe.

My older sisters were more obliging. They still considered themselves Catholics, even though they had given up going to church long ago. They told the bishop everything they thought he wanted to hear, and probably more, and I'm sure he immediately dismissed their testimonies as frivolous and insincere since, as far as I knew, none of them had kept in touch with Marilee since she left for Haiti.

However, my mother proved to be a more worthy informant. She and Marilee had long shared in the church-going experience, and it was my mother's faith, albeit more traditional than it was philosophical, that had turned Marilee on to God so many years ago. My mother referred the bishop to Father Joseph Fitzpatrick, who had baptized Marilee and seen her through her first Communion and reconciliation and confirmation as a young girl.

And as it turned out, my mother came from a long line of devotees. Her mother's father, my great-grandfather, had been the vicar-general for the Bishop of Monte Mario, just outside Vatican City. In fact, he was still remembered well by several of the elder clergymen for his incredible kindness and charity.

Of course, Rasima Rasima was thrilled.

In her book, she writes, "When I learned of Marilee's relation to the good vicar-general of Monte Mario, I had no doubt the Vatican would take my request more seriously. After all, the vicar-general had been considered briefly for sainthood himself some years ago."

And what did my dear old father have to say about Marilee? What could he say? By the time the bishop got around to interviewing him, he was dead from cardiac arrest.

Maybe there is a God.

Upon the conclusion of the investigation in 2022, about the same time Greta was giving it to Norman McCredie in the bedrooms of some of the best real estate in San Francisco, Bishop Carlo Devicchio submitted his report to the Congregation for the Causes of Saints, and Sister Marilee Lorenzo of San Francisco was deemed "Venerable," the first major step to sainthood.

"A huge victory for the Nuns of Borgo Vittorio," Thomas A. Rhett writes.

Now all Rasima Rasima had to do was drum up a couple of miracles.

CHAPTER 23

I HAVE JUST HEARD from Duncan. He writes:

Dear Jim,

I am pleased to hear you are enjoying your holiday in Paris. I have only been once, to visit my sister at university. Paris is too big and too noisy for me. Nevertheless, I imagine a worldly traveler such as yourself will find the city agreeable, particularly this time of year, when the weather is so warm.

In answer to your question regarding Dr. Elijah Mitzner: yes, Greta and I knew him growing up in Antwerp. He was a close friend of the family, and our childhood doctor. His family came to work on our farm at the end of the Second World War in 1944. He was only two years old.

The Mitzners originated in Poland. After Germany invaded in 1939, they were transferred to a ghetto in Lodz where they lived until 1941. During a raid in 1941, the family was separated, and Freda Mitzner, Dr. Mitzner's mother, was taken to Dachau. Her husband, Isaac Mitzner, was taken to Auschwitz and killed.

Dr. Mitzner was born in the Dachau concentration camp in 1942. His mother managed to hide him from the Nazis with the help of the other women in her barracks until their release in 1944.

After the war, the surviving Mitzners, who were numbered at about five or six, emigrated to Belgium, where my grandfather gave them work as farmhands. They lived out of a small house in the east orchard, and they earned their keep as fruit pickers and sheepherders.

Dr. Mitzner went on to study medicine, and he later worked at the hospital in Antwerp. Our mother sent us over to the Mitzner place whenever either of us had a runny nose or a scraped knee.

When my father died in 2000, my mother sold off most

of the land, keeping only our small cottage and a few surrounding acres, which you have seen for yourself. Elijah moved his family to California, where he opened a private practice in Palo Alto, and from there I think you know the rest.

I have not thought about Dr. Mitzner in a very long time. I recall his mother telling us how she very nearly strangled him to keep him from crying at night in the death camp. And sometimes she had to go days without food so he could eat. Some of the other women in the camp put aside bits of bread for the child, and they took turns caring for him. And sometimes he had to be left alone for many hours, tucked neatly away between two mattresses. It is a wonder he survived at all.

When Dr. Mitzner passed away in 2030, his family wrote to ask if he could be buried here on the farm, where he grew up. Forty-three members of the Mitzner clan showed up for the ceremony; they came from all over the world. When the ceremony was over, every single one of them shook my hand and thanked me graciously for what my grandfather had done. He had given the Mitzners refuge and a livelihood. He had given them posterity.

I am sorry I never got out to California. I would like to

have seen Greta and Dr. Mitzner again before they died. I like to think sometimes of Greta, whose ashes have melted into the soil, and of Dr. Mitzner, who rests under the big chestnut tree, and I like to imagine them as they were when I was a child: Greta with a skinned knee and Dr. Mitzner holding her hand as he examines the scrape through his big browline glasses.

That's how they will always be to me. That's how they will stay.

Very much your dear old friend.

Duncan

CHAPTER 24

FIRST IT WAS THE SCHOOLTEACHER in Buenos Aires who claimed Sister Marilee Lorenzo appeared to her in a dream. Then it was the girl in South Africa with stigmata. And then there was the blind beggar in Taipei who prayed to Sister Marilee Lorenzo and subsequently regained his sight.

Rasima Rasima submitted each of these claims to the Vatican committee appointed to review Marilee's case and was met each time with skepticism and a subsequent rejection.

The schoolteacher in Buenos Aires had a history of drug abuse. The girl in South Africa was a cutter. The blind beggar in Taipei was a scam artist.

Then a letter came from a poor fisherman in Nova Scotia. He claimed that whenever he tied a small strand of white ribbon to the bow of his little dinghy, mackerels and trout started jumping out of the sea and into the boat. The ribbon, he claimed, came from the funeral wreath that had adorned Marilee's casket at her memorial service in 2017.

Rasima Rasima writes in her book:

When I arrived in the village of Sambro, Nova Scotia, Mr. Puttner invited me into his kitchen and showed me a freezer full of fish. He laid the ribbon out on the table. It was no more than ten inches long, and frayed at the ends. I examined the artifact closely. All the flower arrangements for the memorial service had come from the Flower Emporium on Eighteenth Street in San Francisco. Sister Ellen Roderick had chosen the ribbon herself from a catalogue. This was indeed the same ribbon.

Then Mr. Puttner took me out on his little dinghy. He tied the ribbon to the tow ring at the bow. No more than five minutes had passed before dozens of fish began leaping out of the water and into the keel.

I called Bishop Carlo Devicchio directly, and he came out at once to investigate the claim. On our first trip out to sea with the bishop, only two fish jumped into the keel. "Surely this cannot be the miracle you speak of," said the bishop. But the next morning, Mr. Puttner took us out again. This time we counted 148 fish in the keel. At the end of four days' time, we had amassed a total of 753 fish. However, on the fifth day, there were only eight fish. And on the sixth day, there were none.

The vicar-general, who was also there, caught the whole episode on his camera phone. The footage made headlines, and Rasima Rasima was hopeful. She writes:

> This time we had our miracle. John 6:10 tells how Jesus fed the five thousand with fish. This had to be a sign from God.

But then all sorts of similar YouTube videos began circulating on the Internet. Apparently fish all around the world were known to leap into boats from time to time when their waters were disturbed. The Bureau of Fishing and Game called the phenomenon "fish bombing."

The Vatican promptly dismissed the case.

They issued a statement:

> When Jesus fed the five thousand, he did so with only five loaves of bread and two fish. Food was scarce, and

the people were starving. What good is it if fish leap into a boat in a part of the world where fish are plentiful and hunger is nonexistent? We recognize the good fortune of the fisherman of Sambro, but we cannot justly call it a miracle when so many others are starving the world over.

Thomas A. Rhett writes, "Following this disappointment, Rasima Rasima disappeared from the public eye for several years. Her followers claim she spent her days absorbed in heavenly contemplation."

Then in 2030, a young girl in Somalia, no more than ten years old, claimed a woman had appeared to her in a copse on the outskirts of her village. The apparition had pointed to the roots of a tree and said, "Drink." The girl, frightened, ran all the way home and told her mother. The next day, the village priest was summoned, and together they went to the place where the girl had seen the apparition.

The girl pointed to the spot on the ground where the woman had said to drink. There was nothing more than sunbaked earth. The priest began to dig. Suddenly water began to bubble up from the ground.

The village had no water source of its own. The women were forced to walk twenty miles for water to the nearest river, which was regularly patrolled by vigilantes and thieves. Many of the women were either injured or harmed along the journey, or beaten and raped at the river. The new spring promised to quench the thirst of the village and end the perilous pilgrimage for water.

The village priest wrote to Rome. Bishop Carlo Devicchio was sent to Somalia to investigate.

"No doubt Rasima Rasima beat the bishop to the scene," Thomas A. Rhett writes. "How else could she be sure that the young girl knew it was Sister Marilee Lorenzo she had seen in the copse and not some other saint or deity?"

Rasima Rasima writes in her book:

> I had already been at the village three days when the good bishop finally arrived. I turned over dozens of written testimonies I had gathered from the villagers that I had translated myself. The young girl, whom I had interviewed extensively, told the bishop precisely what she told me: Sister Marilee Lorenzo had shown her the way to the spring.

In 2031 the Vatican sanctified the miracle, now known in popular culture as the Miracle of the Spring, and the Venerable Marilee Lorenzo was elevated to the status of "Blessed," one step away from "Saint."

The Miracle of the Spring was highly politicized, as 2031 marked the beginning of the Global Water Crisis. Between 2031 and 2034, the price of water around the globe increased hundredfold in urban areas, and became virtually priceless in developing nations. The year 2031 saw the final drop of water siphoned from the Ogallala Aquifer, which had vitalized the American Midwest following the Dust Bowl. In 2033 the Nubian Sandstone Aquifer in Northern Africa went dry after nearly two decades of widespread industrial farming. And the final blow came in 2034 when a study by the United Nations reported the disappearance of over two hundred rivers and streams worldwide.

The global response was frenzied. Many developing countries, deep in debt and lacking the infrastructure to support a national crisis, went to war for water. The superpowers, countries like the United States and China, paid increasingly higher prices for freshwater, and raced to harness unclaimed glacial ice in arctic territories. Meanwhile, in Europe and Asia, research continued on the desalinization techniques that had been all but abandoned at the turn of the century in favor of groundwater drilling.

When the average price of water in the United States nearly centupled in 2034, the American Southwest could no longer afford to support the millions of people who had settled the desert regions of Southern California and Las Vegas. Tinseltown and Sin City fell into economic ruin, and, consequently, Northern California seceded from the south, creating two new states now known as New Shasta and Villanova. The gory details of the split are outlined in historian Paul Elroy's *New York Times* best seller, *The California Water Crisis of 2034*.

My sisters, who were then living in LA, scattered to all corners of the country, hoping to escape the drought and conflict. My mother, being rich and stubborn, decided to stick it out in Malibu, paying exorbitant prices to maintain the life of country clubs, spas, and lawn parties to which she had grown accustomed. She died in 2046, the same year Matzick Geihzko, a PhD student in Moscow, designed a desalinization method that could convert up to two hundred gallons of seawater to freshwater every second.

That's where the water I'm drinking now comes from: one of the Geihzko plants off the coast of Brittany, France. And when I go home to New Shasta, I will draw my water from a Geihzko plant that was once an oil rig off the Santa Barbara coast.

It's not cheap. But it's a start. It's a start.

So imagine in 2030, a little girl in northern Somalia

discovers a freshwater spring in a dry copse just on the eve of a global water crisis.

Who wouldn't call that a miracle?

CHAPTER 25

IN PAUL ELROY'S most recent book, *The Greater Depression*, for which he was awarded the Pulitzer Prize in 2055, he describes the years ensuing the California Water Crisis as "the darkest years since the Dark Ages."

They were dark years for me, too, but not for the same reasons as everybody else. I was rich, and rich people could afford to eat and drink and sleep in comfort, even with the world falling apart, even in the Greater Depression.

Nevertheless, I had my lows like everybody else. For me those dark years saw the deaths of all four of my sisters to heart disease. And then my mother, too, of liver failure.

That was also about the time the Catholic Church pulled Marilee out of the ground and put her on display in a glass coffin for all the world to see. Standard procedure, they told me, for candidates in line for sainthood.

Her corpse remained on display in the Grace Cathedral for about a year, and then they asked me if I had any objections to her going to Rome.

I'd never objected to Marilee going anywhere before. So off Marilee went to Rome, where she remains a major tourist attraction to this day.

Those were also the years the kids moved away to college: Eliza to Ann Arbor and Spencer to New York City. Only Kendra Ann stayed in San Francisco, but the SF Gators had her flying all over the country for basketball games every other weekend.

Meanwhile, I was all alone in that big house. Except for Greta's ghost rattling around somewhere in the walls.

I bought a German shepherd in 2037, the same year Kendra Ann moved out. I named him T-Rex. T-Rex was stolen out of the yard less than a year later. Incidentally, that upset me more than any of my sisters' deaths. Probably because I knew T-Rex was going to end up a soufflé for some starving family.

Lots of dogs and cats were being kidnapped for food back in those days.

"Common household pets had more to fear than anyone," Elroy writes in *The Greater Depression*. "The population of house cats dropped fifty-seven percent in the decade following the California Water Crisis. The population of domesticated dogs dropped seventy-two percent."

I never ate dog or cat. I didn't need to. I had money to buy rarities like beef and pork and fish. But the rest of the world was hungry. As a matter of fact, the rest of the world was *starving*.

What had happened?

In 2034, when US farmers already had their hands full with the Global Water Crisis, and when the US government was spending billions of dollars to channel water from the Pacific Northwest to the thirsty states in the Midwest, a new terror struck the breadbasket of America.

Its official name was *Sangoria minoris*, but the media called it Fetter's Rot after the biologist Robert A. Fetter, who was the first to identify the virus. It originated, they think, in Northern California, now New Shasta, around the Sacramento Delta area. And it spread quickly across the Sierras and into the Mississippi River region, and, finally, around the world.

It affected corn, primarily, and some varieties of wheat and barley. Before the corn or wheat or barley could fully ripen, the stalk would wither and rot, folding over on itself like a lawn chair. This gave the dying vegetable the appearance of a man with his head slumped onto his chest. On a trip down Interstate 5 to visit my mother in 2036, all I could see for miles and miles were the slumped-over silhouettes of what looked like regiments of narcoleptic scarecrows.

The food industry was devastated. They had spent so many years planting the same old monocultures and GMOs that the crops had become virtually indistinct from one another. There was no stopping Fetter's Rot from taking out every single one of these vegetal clones in a matter of months.

Poof goes the world!

Of course this led to hunger everywhere. Nothing to eat. Nothing to drink. A census report showed the world population dipping for the first time since World War Two.

The sheer scope of Fetter's Rot is best described in Elroy's book:

> Among the 198 recognized countries of the world, 197 reported at least one confirmed case of Fetter's Rot. The only sovereign state to remain unaffected was Vatican City, the only country in the world with no agriculture whatsoever.

The first to starve to death were the cows and pigs and

chickens and farmed fish, which survived primarily off a diet of corn and grain. No way were they getting dinner while the rest of us starved. Except for a few small ranches with deep pockets, the entire meat-packing industry went *ker-plop*.

The cost of meat skyrocketed. Paul Elroy writes, "The US Census reported some fifty-two million vegetarians in the country in 2030. That number ballooned to two hundred fifty million by 2040."

Then in 2041, an 8.9-magnitude earthquake leveled South Central Los Angeles. My mother slept through the whole thing. The earthquake lasted forty-eight seconds. My mother was napping on the sofa after a long brunch at the country club, and when she awoke, she found all the glass windows shattered and her swimming pool empty.

My mother was nearly thirty miles from the epicenter of the quake. Nevertheless, she suffered something like $20,000 in property damage.

The rest of Los Angeles was decimated. The president of the United States, a man by the name of Stuart Trump, of the Trump family, declared a national emergency, and aid trickled in from whichever countries still had any money or food to spare, namely China.

In *The Greater Depression*, Elroy concludes that the Villanova earthquake of 2041 marks the moment that

Hollywood got out of Los Angeles for good. Hollywood producers had already moved filming out to Vancouver for the tax breaks. But following the California Water Crisis, and the secession of the North, and then finally the Villanova earthquake of 2041, every major motion picture company hightailed it to Canada, taking all of the glitz and glam of the American Dream with them.

Every empire must fall.

But it wasn't the Villanova earthquake that brought the world to its knees; major cities had suffered natural disasters before. Nor was it the Global Water Crisis, which spiked the cost of water to nearly the price of oil. Those were not the kickers. It was a strain of tiny little microorganisms that seemed to move across the globe like an apocalyptic plague of locusts. *Sangoria minoris.* Fetter's Rot.

Paul Elroy writes, "The world was in a state of emergency. Never in the history of humankind had every corner of the earth been so hungry. Who could come to the rescue now, when everyone on the planet needed rescuing? The best thing, some said, would be to send an SOS to the stars and hope for an alien race to intervene."

But it wasn't an alien race that intervened.

It was Rowan Krasimir.

CHAPTER 26

WHEN THE BIG ONE struck in 2041, Rasima Rasima got her second miracle. She was in New Delhi, at the opening of another Marilee Lorenzo Free Clinic, when news reached her of an 8.9-magnitude earthquake in the heart of South Central Los Angeles.

"My first concern," Rasima Rasima writes in her book, "was the safety of the orphaned children of South Gate, a municipality of Los Angeles County where we had just opened an orphanage only a year before and where the earthquake was said to have taken the largest toll. Communications were down, and air traffic was at a standstill. We simply had to sit and wait for news to come over the wire."

News came, all right. The city of South Gate had crumbled like the walls of Jericho. Los Angeles had long been famous for its elaborate network of fault lines, which criss-crossed the region like the cracks in a shattered windshield. However, geologists had missed a major thrust fault that coursed through the heart of South Gate like a pulmonary artery. They later called it the Tweedy Fault for its almost perfect alignment with South Gate's most prominent street, Tweedy Boulevard.

The Tweedy Fault showed no mercy. Initial reports had the death toll at nearly fifteen thousand, with another twenty thousand still missing. Thirty thousand homes were destroyed in addition to another twenty thousand commercial and municipal buildings. Rescue crews were working around the clock to pull survivors from the wreckage.

Then news came of a miracle. Amid all the death and destruction, one building had been spared: South Gate's Marilee Lorenzo Children's Home. Standing almost directly atop the fault line, the children's home had taken the brunt of the impact, yet suffered virtually no damage. Helicopter footage showed the children's home standing perfectly intact amid the wreckage, like a life raft in a churning sea.

What's more, reports from inside the building stated no one had been injured or harmed, and that most of the napping children had slept through the quake, just as my eighty-five-year-old mother in Malibu had after a brunch heavy in scotch and tonic.

The Marilee Lorenzo Children's Home transferred the children to a temporary facility in Reseda, away from the worst of the destruction. The director of the children's home then turned the building over to emergency crews, and within twenty-four hours, the children's home became the beating heart and homestead of the Red Cross efforts.

It couldn't have gone more smoothly if Marilee had orchestrated the whole thing herself.

Rasima Rasima made it out to Los Angeles a week later. She paid a visit to the orphans who had survived unscathed. Then she joined the Red Cross relief efforts. She was, after all, a two-time earthquake veteran.

Three months later Bishop Carlo Devicchio came out to Los Angeles to see for himself what kind of miracle had occurred there. Then in 2042, the Vatican made my sister a saint—Saint Marilee Lorenzo of San Francisco.

Theological scholar Thomas A. Rhett writes in *The Origins of a Saint*:

> It would be hard to deny the miraculous nature of the events of South Gate in 2041. The iconic image, circulated in the press, of the perfectly preserved children's hospital has become an enduring emblem in the Catho-

lic Church of God's great mercy. However, many critics are quick to point out that the building was less than a year old; it was the most recent construction in South Gate by some twenty years. Consequently, it was equipped with the latest and greatest advances in retrofit technology. So, some ask, miracle of God or miracle of engineering?

I don't know how Marilee would answer. But she'd most certainly say it was no miracle of her own.

Nevertheless, an article in *The New York Times* recently stated that the papacy plans to assign Saint Marilee Lorenzo patronage over earthquakes.

Magnum Opus.

Things in Los Angeles have improved some in the decade since the earthquake, but Villanova is still the most economically unstable state in the union. Repeated efforts to reunite Shasta and Villanova have failed, namely because the North has no interest in shackling itself to the debt and poverty of an economy with nothing to offer.

No water. No agriculture. Not even a decent Hollywood film every now and then.

All the good movies come from Canada now.

So be it.

Speaking of movies, I just went to see a picture at the Cinéma Gaumont Parnasse on rue d'Odessa. Everything in Paris is screened in its original language with French sub-titles, and this particular film was in English. Canadian English.

Incidentally, the movie was about a writer who stays home all day pumping out crime thrillers. His wife is a lawyer at a big firm, and they have a hunky-dory apple pie relationship with two kids, a dog named Ralph, and a cat named Whiskers.

Original.

The writer in the movie has started a new novel about a guy who suspects his wife is cheating on him, and winds up in a twisted game of cat and mouse trying to root out the truth. His protagonist's name is Peter Holt.

It's a story inside a story, you see.

Now, as the writer gets further along in his story, he starts to notice little oddities in his own life, like an extra key on his wife's key ring, or a funny smell on her collar, which are precisely the sorts of things the guy in his novel finds suspicious.

With the kids at school and his wife at work all the time,

the writer spends his days alone in his big house, and this starts to drive him a little batty. Between bouts of writing, he starts to wander around the house looking for clues, suspecting, as does the character in his book, that his wife has been unfaithful.

This goes on for some time, with lots of long shots of the writer staring at a necklace or a ribbon and imagining a handsome stranger putting it on or taking it off.

The writer begins to suspect his neighbor, a single dad with whom his wife coordinates carpools for the kids, of seducing his wife. The paranoid writer grows hostile toward his wife and their neighbor, believing the two of them to be in on some harebrained conspiracy that mirrors perfectly what Peter Holt is experiencing in the novel.

The writer starts acting really nutty, but it isn't until his wife takes a peek at the finished manuscript that she realizes the danger they're all in. The last line of the novel reads, "In a fit of jealousy and rage, Peter Holt pointed the gun and pulled the trigger."

Boom!

She hears a gunshot from upstairs and rushes in to find the writer dead on the floor with a gun in his mouth.

The end.

Pretty morbid stuff. Subsequently, we learn that the wife

was never having an affair, even though her husband suspected she was.

In my experience it works the other way around—the husband never suspected his wife was having an affair, even though she actually was.

In both stories someone ends up dead.

The movie was called *Everything is Rosé*, a reference to the pink stain the writer finds on his wife's blouse that leads him to suspect her of boozing with another man.

Incidentally, it was a bottle of rosé that finally warmed Greta up to me so many years ago when we met again in Paris.

She was a bit of a lightweight, Greta.

Happy Happy Happy Message Runners, Inc. sent me back to Paris in July of 2011. Back then July was the hottest time of the year in Paris. It happens to be July 2056 as I write, and it's raining outside. That's normal, they tell me, nowadays.

I didn't know if I'd see Greta again, especially after she'd sent some lackey in her place the last time I'd been over. Nevertheless, I came prepared. I had on a pair of tapered slacks, a white button-down, and oxfords. I'd even cut my hair for the occasion, which, as anyone will tell you, is not my favorite thing to do.

When I found her, she was sitting on the edge of the river Seine, her legs dangling over the embankment and her head tilted to the sun. She wore a wide-brimmed hat and big tortoiseshell sunglasses, a long summer dress, golden sandals, and a light-gray sweater that had slipped off one shoulder to reveal translucent skin polka-dotted with freckles.

The red cooler was to her right. A picnic basket to her left.

She pretended not to notice me when I sat down, the picnic basket between us. I cleared my throat. She looked over her shoulder at me and then back again at some fixed spot on the opposite bank. A dinner cruise floated by, floodlights blazing.

"Looks like an alien spaceship," I said.

"Maybe it is," she said, "here to conquer the earth."

"Or maybe just on vacation," I said, "visiting the most beautiful city in the universe."

"You don't think they have beautiful cities where they come from?" she asked.

"Maybe they do," I said, "but there's something romantic about Paris. Maybe it's all the movies."

"They watch our movies on other planets?" she asked.

"Oh sure," I said. "We make the best movies in the universe. Have you ever seen a Martian film?"

"Can't say that I have."

"Complete garbage," I said. "Even worse than German expressionism."

She let out a little puff of air that I thought might be something like a laugh. I was encouraged.

"You brought a picnic," I said.

"Have it if you want," she replied, pushing the basket toward me.

"Are you as hungry as I am?" I asked.

She didn't respond. I rummaged through the basket.

"Wine, strawberries, cheese," I said, listing the contents.

"Rosé," she said. "From Provence."

"This is for us?"

"For you," she said, "since you're always so hungry."

Then she started to stand.

"Wait!" I said. "Aren't you at least going to have a glass of rosé with me?"

"I don't think so."

"One glass," I begged.

"I have somewhere to be."

"But there are two glasses here," I protested. "Why would you pack two glasses if you weren't planning on staying?"

She stared into the water and didn't say anything for a while. The sun was setting over La Défense. The last rays of light skipped over the lazy water.

"I saw you at the Jardin des Plantes," she said finally.

"What?"

"Last time you were here," she said, "I saw you."

I didn't respond. My hands were sweating. I fumbled with the bottle of rosé, popped the cork, and poured us each a glass.

"After that, Rowan wanted to meet you himself," she continued.

"Yeah," I said, "I saw him."

"He says you've been in this business a long time and you've never asked any questions."

"I've always thought we were trafficking drugs or organs or something," I said.

"And you wouldn't have cared," she asked, "if we were trafficking drugs or organs?"

"I just didn't want to know," I replied sheepishly.

"Interesting rationale."

I sipped my wine.

"So what's really in the coolers?" I asked.

"Sandwiches."

"Come on," I said. "If it's not drugs or organs, then why can't you tell me?"

"Part of the plan, Stan," she said, feigning an American accent.

"What do you do at the Jardin des Plantes?" I asked.

"Research."

"Could you be a little more specific?"

"No," she said, "not until Rowan gives you clearance."

She was sipping delicately at the rosé.

"What does that mean?" I demanded.

"Never mind," she said, "I shouldn't have said anything."

All along the bank of the river, other small groups were gathering with bottles of beer and wine. A few teenagers had brought bongo drums, and they set a steady beat as a few of their friends chanted along.

Greta offered me a strawberry.

"Thanks," I said.

"So is this your only job," she asked, "working for Rowan?"

"Yeah."

"And you're happy?"

I shrugged.

"So what do you do in the meantime?" she asked.

"I dunno," I said. "Hang out. Invest in stocks."

"You have a girlfriend?" she asked.

"No."

There was a long pause.

"Can I give you a pointer?" she said.

"Sure."

"I prefer champagne." And, with that, she got up and walked away.

We were married a year later, after a sum total of eleven dates, if that's what you want to call our little meet-ups along the Seine. It was sort of a shotgun wedding. Greta had to get out of Paris for a while, keep a low profile. Rowan offered her a job in the States. Our marriage license expedited the whole visa process considerably.

By that time I knew all of her little secrets. I knew she was forced to resign from her position at the Jardin des Plantes in March 2012 for the suspected misuse of state-funded resources. Fortunately, the administration didn't order an investigation; they accepted Greta's resignation and hinted that her career in state-funded research was dead in the water.

I also knew she was on some sort of security watch list in North and South Korea for trespassing and the trafficking of goods across the North-South border. A friend of hers in the

French Ministry of Foreign Affairs alluded to the fact that her name had surfaced in a file that was circulating around the ministry, and that she had better get out of the country tout de suite.

We were married on April 20, 2012. We left for the United States the following day. The next time I returned to France was in 2039 for the Lambert-Keaton trials, where I testified against my then-deceased wife.

Yes, I would tell the prosecutor, *Greta admitted to trespassing onto North Korean territory a handful of times.*

No, she was not a communist spy.

No, she did not have any contact with anyone in the Kim Jong-il administration. As far as I know, she did not have contact with anyone at all.

Yes, a biologist.

To study indigenous plant species, I think.

I'm sure she was aware of the risks.

Yes, the date rings a bell.

She said she was delayed for a number of days.

Yes, in North Korea.

Apparently there was a warrant out for her arrest. At least that's what she told me.

Not technically. I believe she was detained by the South

Korean authorities at the border.

No, they let her go.

I think a bribe.

I'm just telling you what she told me.

I have no reason to disbelieve it.

Yes, she brought back a few things.

Sandwiches, I think.

Well, if you already know what else, then—

Fine. Yes. That, too.

If you say so, but I'm pretty sure that isn't a crime.

Have I ever been to North Korea? Well...

CHAPTER 27

I HAVE JUST gotten off the phone with Eliza. Duncan has died. I am taking the train to Belgium tomorrow. There will be somebody there to go over the specifics of his will. The farm and all that precious water underneath has been left to me. Good gracious.

They're going to cremate Duncan's body and spread it over the farm, just like we did with Greta. Spencer is going with me, and Eugene is going to stay in Paris with the girls. We'll only be a few days. Then we'll let the attorneys handle the rest.

It was peaceful, whatever it was. A neighbor to whom Duncan regularly dealt vegetables stopped by yesterday afternoon and found him in his old sofa chair with an almanac in his lap.

Somebody will have to take care of his cat.

He didn't have a microchip.

"A shame," Eliza says, "a real shame."

She took advantage of the occasion to remind me about my appointment next week with Dr. Pierre Lavoie on rue Etienne Marcel.

"Have you been taking a muscle relaxant?" she demanded.

"Yes, yes," I said.

"And you're walking every day? Remember, exercise is important."

"I know."

"A tragedy. A real tragedy."

"He was old," I said. "At least he died peacefully."

"But he didn't have a microchip. No one will ever know his story."

"Not every story needs to be told."

"Says the man writing his memoir."

"I'm writing it for your mother," I said. "She never got to tell *her* story."

There was silence on the other end of the line.

Then, after a long pause, "I don't believe you're writing it for Mom."

"Maybe yes, maybe no."

CHAPTER 28

THINGS GOT PRETTY INTERESTING after that first date on the riverbank with Greta. I didn't know then that her decision to stick around for a glass of rosé wasn't an attempt at flirtation; it was a reconnaissance mission. Rowan Krasimir wanted me for a special operation.

I arrived at the mailbox outside the San Francisco Public Library with the most recent red cooler, which contained, to the best of my knowledge, a tuna sandwich and nothing more, and waited for my contact to show.

It was the kid, Dustin, again. He pulled up on his motorbike at half past ten.

"Get on," he said and tossed me a helmet.

"Are you kidding?"

"No, Rowan wants to meet you," he said. "Hurry, we're late."

"I'm not going anywhere with you on that thing."

"Come on," Dustin said, cracking a devilish smile. "You scared?"

I shrugged.

He revved the engine menacingly.

"Fine," I said and climbed aboard. "Where are we going?"

"You'll see," he said and slammed on the gas.

We went hurtling toward Market Street, and I clung to the kid's jacket for dear life. The cooler was in one hand. My other arm was thrown around his waist. He wasn't big, maybe 125 pounds, and I felt like any grip I got on his slight frame wasn't enough.

"Rowan's cool," the kid yelled over his shoulder.

The wind was rushing by, making it almost impossible to hear.

"Apparently you did something right," he continued. "He's giving you clearance."

"Keep your eyes on the road," I said.

The kid laughed, "Okay, boss."

We zoomed down Eighth Street, dodging cars and darting around buses. Then we were on the Bay Bridge, humming along with the rest of the trans-bay commuters.

"See that?" Dustin said. "They're almost done with the new bridge."

"Yeah," I managed.

We didn't speak again for some time. He took Interstate 580 south for a while, through Oakland and San Leandro. Then he veered east, following the snaking track of BART, which zipped alongside the freeway, taunting me with its brightly lit cabins and indoor seating.

Somewhere just outside Livermore, we pulled off the freeway, onto a quiet country road that wound through the canyons of the east hills. The city had fallen away to grassy hummocks spotted with grazing cattle and large white wind turbines that stood like giant sentinels along the ridge.

"Most of our power comes from those turbines," the kid said. "In case something happens, we'll always have wind."

In case something happens?

I hadn't seen another vehicle on the road for some time when finally we pulled off onto a dirt track that led to a barbwire fence policed by a little industrial guardhouse.

A young guard greeted us at the gate. Dustin presented a badge and then added, "He should be on the list," then to me, "Give him your license."

I fumbled through my pockets for my wallet.

The guard scrolled through a computer, found my name, glanced at my license, and then printed out a yellow pass with my name, the date, and time.

"Your pass is good 'til six o'clock," the guard said. "Then all visitors must vacate the premises."

"Yeah," Dustin said, "we know the drill."

The gate slid back, and Dustin motored through. Then he pressed the throttle and raced up a steep hill, atop of which sat a low, squat building surrounded by several small bunkers and what looked like two or three glass domes.

"Is this InfraGen Tech?" I asked as we dismounted.

"Not quite," said the kid. "Welcome to the SHEM Project."

CHAPTER 29

TODAY WE WENT through Duncan's things. There are a few items of notable value, a sterling silver pocket watch, a gold wedding band that must have been his father's, and an enameled music box from the nineteenth century. Those he bequeathed to Eliza, Spencer, and Kendra Ann, respectively. The rest of his belongings are up for grabs, and anything that doesn't find a new home with us will be donated to the Salvation Army offices in Antwerp.

Spencer was fascinated by some of Duncan's gardening tools, which have outlasted a century and remain in working order. The instruments have been kept in mint condition, no doubt by Duncan, who was a notorious miser and never bought anything new unless he had no other choice. Most of the relics in his house hail back to the 1940s, when his father modernized the farm after the war.

Spencer intends to take up gardening, so the yard tools were of particular interest to him. I don't see how he plans to get them all through customs without raising hell.

I'm going to raise a few eyebrows myself trying to get Bentley the Stuffed Crow across the border. Bentley wasn't always stuffed. Once he was a real crow filled with blood and guts and sinew. Greta used to tell stories about Bentley: how as children she and Duncan found him wounded in the yard, how they took him in and fed him and nursed him back to health, how he learned to curse in Dutch and French, how he used to get into the pantry and sneak marshmallows, how the neighbor's cat lost an eye in an epic battle of feline versus fowl.

To Greta, Bentley was a legend. A hero! I think that's what Bentley was to Duncan, too.

When Bentley died, they stuffed him with wool and wire and put him on the mantel for display. I promised to take care of Bentley after Duncan died, which makes me the legal custodian of no less than *two* resurrected corpses: a taxi-dermied crow and a sister in a glass coffin.

Go figure.

Tomorrow we will scatter Duncan's ashes on the farm. Today we took a walk around the property so Spencer could see precisely where his mother's ashes wound up. Incidentally, the house and surrounding gardens are precisely as they were thirty-one years ago when I first visited Duncan in 2025. The cottage is still a museum; the garden is flourishing.

However, there was an important addition that caught me quite by surprise, even though I should have expected it. Dr. Elijah Mitzner is buried out there now. He has a simple granite tombstone under the old chestnut tree, just as Duncan described.

Spencer remembers Dr. Mitzner. When we stumbled upon his grave, we stood there for some time, pondering. The sky was gloomy and gray. The world was quiet. There were crows perched all along the telephone wires, and, naturally, I wondered if any of them was any relation to Bentley the Stuffed Crow.

"What do you think?" I asked Spencer after some time had passed.

"Seems as good a place as any to be buried," he said. "I wouldn't mind spending eternity here. It's so peaceful, you know? Way out here, away from the hustle and bustle of the everyday."

"And yet *this was* Duncan's everyday," I said.

We stood there awhile longer. I thought maybe Spencer

was feeling a little of what I felt the first time I came to this faraway place: an immediate sense of my own mortality. Here in the garden, where one thing grows out of the remains of another. How many of these plants, these trees sprang from Greta's ashes?

We went back inside to finish packing up. There I found another surprise. In the kitchen, on the windowsill, was the urn, Greta's urn. It was the same urn I had carried all the way from San Francisco to Antwerp, the same urn Duncan promised to bury in the garden when the ground thawed.

But it was not buried in the garden. It was sitting plainly on the windowsill. It had not moved an inch in all the thirty-one years I'd been away, not an inch since Duncan had rinsed it with water and left it on the windowsill to dry. It looked like it had never been touched.

"It was your mother's," I said to Spencer, who lifted it quite unceremoniously from its resting place and peered inside.

"It's empty," he said.

"What did you expect?"

He shrugged and replaced the lid.

"Should we bring it with us?" he asked.

"I don't know if I want to," I said.

"Eliza will kill us if we don't."

"Are you planning on telling her about it?" I asked.

He shrugged.

"We have some time to think about it," I said. "What do you feel like for dinner?"

"Do they deliver pizza out here?"

CHAPTER 30

MY AGENT, Sam Getz, says I have to get my word count up.

"People don't like to pay a lot of money for a small book," he says. "You can't expect people to take it seriously if you're under eighty thousand words. And for a memoir? Forget it!"

What does it mean that the story of my life doesn't meet the minimum word count?

Ah well. Magnum Opus.

I also heard from my friend and lawyer, Holly Carter. She says we have to sit down when I get back and have a serious discussion if I still plan to go ahead with this brain download.

"We'll have to draw up a whole new will," she said. "You're going to have to leave your future self a little something to live on, that is, in the event that you are, in fact, brought back to life."

"Uh-hum," I said. It sounded like something from *Star Trek*, and even though she was speaking in a very grave tone, I couldn't take her seriously.

"You know you have the option to specify," she continued, "whether or not you'd even want to be revived, and if so, when. That is if they ever get it working right. At the moment they're not even close."

"Uh-hum."

"You are also free to declare, 'For Medical Emergencies Only,'" she went on, "which basically means they'll only use the backup brain if you suffer memory loss or a stroke or some other sort of brain damage. But then again, they're still far from having the technology to do that, and they're not likely to get it up and running in either of our lifetimes. Still, it's just a precaution, even if you don't want to be brought back to life, which I don't think you do. Am I right?"

"Uh-hum."

"Jim!" her voice blared over the receiver. "You have to listen to me! This isn't just some sort of Frankenstein fan-fiction fantasy. This is really happening. When you are through with the procedure, there is going to be a real-life, honest-to-goodness copy of your brain sitting on a microchip somewhere, and heaven knows what could happen if you don't take precautions to protect yourself from fraud or theft or God knows what else!"

"Look, Holly," I said. "You've been my lawyer a long time. And a good one. The best. You got me out of a real mess back in the old days, and so I'm going to just go ahead and do whatever you tell me to do, okay?"

"Then I'm telling you not to get your brain downloaded in the first place."

"I mean after that," I said.

"Well, this isn't my area of expertise, you know." She sounded exasperated. "We didn't have this kind of thing when I was studying law."

"I trust you anyway," I said.

"Listen," she began measuredly, taking a deep breath. "We'll sit down and talk it all through when you get home. I'll bring along a friend who knows a hell of a lot more about this sort of thing than I do, and he'll make sure we don't miss anything. In the meantime, just make sure you mail that chip to Humanity Co. for safekeeping, okay? And, Jim?"

"Yeah?"

"Good luck."

I asked Holly to e-mail over some of the transcripts from the Lambert-Keaton trials since I don't remember a lot of the specifics. After taking the witness stand in Paris in 2039 to testify against my wife, I was summarily handed over to the US attorney general for further questioning.

Apparently *I* shouldn't have been in North Korea either.

They held private hearings. Holly Carter signed on to the case in my defense, thank God. I was lucky. Holly was at the top of her game back then. A thirtysomething powerhouse of a woman with a biting wit and a body to go with it. I sort of had a thing for Holly, still do.

The transcripts she sent over don't convey the actual tone of the trial. On paper, it all looks very dry. Clinical.

The fact of the matter is that it was terrifying. And nasty. I thought I was going to prison for good. And Rowan Krasimir with me. And the kid, Dustin. And Greta's ghost.

Thank God for Holly Carter. And the president of the United States, whom, at the time, was blamed for the California Water Crisis and Fetter's Rot and the collapse of the world economy. Poor guy. All of that was already under way long before he took the oath of office.

I felt bad for the schmuck.

He must have felt pretty bad for me, too. In the end he

commuted my sentence, what little of it there was left to serve when Holly got through with it.

The president felt very indebted to me, you see. A lot of people did. They were chanting my name in the streets outside the courthouse in 2039.

In a surprise turnaround, the president was reelected in 2040. He had been mistakenly credited with driving the country into the ground in 2039, and, soon after, was mistakenly credited with its miraculous recovery, and that was the saving grace of his reelection campaign in 2040. So you can really say *I* was the saving grace of his reelection campaign in 2040.

I couldn't vote for him that year because I was serving time in a federal penitentiary. Nevertheless, he voted for me. He voted for my get-out-of-jail-free card.

The prosecution was a mousy fellow from the offices of the US attorney general. His name was Erich Lambert. Holly Carter was a partner at the legal offices of Keaton Billings & Carter, and, thus, the whole tedious string of hearings, starting on February 22, 2039, in Paris, France, and ending on September 19, 2039, in Washington, DC, were collectively called the Lambert-Keaton trials. Below is some of what I am reported to have said during the hearings:

My name is Jim Lorenzo Frost.

Yes, to Greta Van Bruggen on April 20, 2012.

In Paris.

No, I started working for Happy Happy Happy Message Runners, Inc. in 2006. I didn't meet Greta until 2011.

Yes, she got a job in Livermore, California.

I wouldn't say that, no. We filed all the appropriate documents with the US Department of State. The prosecution has a copy of her visa.

Yes, she did. And she filed for citizenship on January 27, 2025.

No, she died before it went through.

Yes, Rowan Krasimir.

No, I wouldn't say I was employed by him, per se. I was more of an independent contractor.

Fifteen years, on and off. My last assignment was March 11, 2025.

Cash, yes.

For the particular mission under investigation? Fifty grand.

Oh, sorry. Fifty thousand US dollars. Is that better?

I suppose that does sound like a lot. But, ask yourself, how much would it take to persuade you to go to North Korea for five days?

Yes, five days.

No, it was a perfectly legitimate tour company.

Koryo Tours.

They are based out of Beijing. They escort tourists into North Korea. It's a five-day, all-inclusive vacation package. Eighteen hundred dollars, I think. They provide you with accommodation, food, and transportation.

Our guide? He told us to call him Mr. Mok.

I don't remember the names of the other guides.

Yes, two other Americans.

No, I had never met them before the trip.

No, they had no affiliation with Rowan Krasimir.

No, it was just me.

With Greta? That would have been nice, but Greta couldn't go.

Well, as you yourself already know, she was on the Koreans' radar. They were on the lookout for her. So Rowan grounded her.

Yes, grounded. That's what Rowan says when he has to pull an agent off a mission.

No, I was never grounded.

I wasn't an agent. I was what they called a "sandwich guy."

That just means I ran deliveries. A middleman, to throw

off the scent.

No, I didn't know anything about it for years. I just did my job, took the money, and didn't ask questions. I was the ideal sandwich guy. I should have won Sandwich Guy of the Year.

No, sorry, that was a joke.

North Korea?

That was in August of 2011, I think.

Yeah, I suppose you could call it a promotion. But I didn't consider myself a quote-unquote agent.

By definition, yes.

Okay, yes. In that one particular instance—yes, I guess I was an agent.

No, never again.

No, she never went on another mission either. She worked as a researcher at InfraGen Tech after that. I already went over all of this with the French Ministry of Justice.

Fine. But may I have a glass of water?

I've already said North Korea was my only mission.

As an agent, yes.

North Korea, yes. Listen, if you'd like to tell me how you want me to say it, I'm perfectly willing to cooperate.

Very well then. I acted as an agent on one and only one

occasion. On said occasion, I was sent to North Korea. Is that better?

You're welcome.

After that, I went back to being a sandwich guy.

North Korea? It was nice.

I'm not trying to be funny. I'm telling you the truth. It was nice. At least what we got to see of it.

No, you have to stay with an escort the whole time.

No, they don't let you leave the hotel.

No, not without an escort.

No, of course not.

No. You can't go anywhere on your own.

I was never on my own.

I didn't have to be alone to complete my mission.

Somebody just gave it to me.

I don't know. Some guy I'd never seen before.

Of course I was expecting it. What kind of agent would I be if I wasn't expecting it? Everything was prearranged, as Rowan has already testified.

Who? Some Korean guy in a metro station.

No, I didn't catch his name. I barely got a look at his face. There wasn't time to do anything except stuff the thing into my pocket.

We did not exchange any other communication. He

bumped into me in the station, slipped the baggie into my hand, and hurried off.

No, that was it.

I guess that was the second day.

After that? I finished the tour, of course. What else could I do?

Photographs? Sometimes, yes. But the guides delete any pictures they don't like.

Souvenirs? A couple. But they go through everything before you leave the country.

Oh, that was the easy part. I put it in an ice cooler.

Yes, an ice cooler.

Of course they searched it.

Well if I told you that, I'd be spoiling the fun, wouldn't I?

I'm sorry, Your Honor.

Show you? Do you have an ice cooler?

This is one from InfraGen Tech? That's perfect. Here, give it to me.

All right, let me just...There you go. See?

Yes, well it wouldn't register on a metal detector, would it?

That's what the sandwich is for.

Yes, but you would never know. It's very clever, isn't it?

Well as far as I can tell, nothing about it is technically illegal.

Oh. That.

No, it's not mine. Well, it belonged to me. But it's not my real passport.

Yes, that is my picture.

You want me to read it aloud?

The name on the passport reads, "Alex Whittier."

My name is Jim Lorenzo Frost.

The maximum sentence for forgery of a US passport is fifteen years in a federal penitentiary. The maximum sentence for tax evasion is five years plus a quarter million in fines. I was sentenced to three years with minimal fines. Thanks to the cunning of Holly Carter.

I was released in less than sixteen months. Thanks to the clemency of the president of the United States.

He'll go down in history as the president who got us out of the Dark Ages. For a man who was blamed for lobotomizing California, that's a pretty decent epitaph.

I'll go down in history as the unlikely hero who saved the world. Just goes to show that you can't count your chickens—*ever.*

CHAPTER 31

THE WHOLE CLAN took a field trip to the FedEx center in Quartier de la Madeleine this morning. Eugene is done with the first draft of his book, and his agent wants him to send a hard copy via FedEx, since he doesn't trust the Internet, or the US post office, for that matter. Eugene's agent fears the government is tracking his every move. He used to be a member of the California Secessionist Party, or so Eugene tells me.

My so-called agent, Sam Getz, won't deal in anything *but* e-mail. He says it's the greatest tool an agent has. "It's a great way to tell people what you really think without having to wait around to see the look on their faces," he said to me once. But he recently said he doesn't want to hear from me again until I've got at least eighty thousand words.

"You're a *hero*, Jim!" he said. "You've got to give your readers something weighty they can really hold in their hands. That's what the people who read this kind of shit really want."

I just want to know who the hell thinks they've got eighty thousand words worth a damn to say about themselves?

This morning we also FedExed a package for Maggie, who used her allowance to purchase a large mounted watercolor for fifty-five euros from a locally acclaimed street artist named Charles Gaubourg. She has something of her grandmother's appetite for art, it seems.

The watercolor is shipping to their Manhattan loft, where a neighbor has agreed to sign for it.

I packed a few things for Eliza in a separate box destined for California. It was a fifty-euro surcharge to send the package express. But Eliza insisted.

"You don't want your brain bouncing around in the back of a pickup truck as it hits every house in the Tri-Valley area," she said to me on the phone after the procedure was done. Finished. Kaput. I hadn't yet made it out of the ersatz offices of Dr. Pierre Lavoie; the anesthesia was still thick in my bloodstream when she called. "Get that microchip on a direct flight to San Francisco. I won't leave this house until the FedEx guy knocks on my door."

Did I mention that Eliza doesn't have a job? Her husband is paid big bucks to travel all over the world negotiating water trades.

Eliza added, "And make sure you get a tracking number. *Okay, Dad?*"

I packed a few other surprises for Eliza, partly for my own amusement and partly because I can't bear to have sentimental knickknacks lying around our Paris apartment, stirring up ghosts.

Can you guess?

Yes, Greta's urn is in there, to satisfy my dear little Eliza's lifelong wish to have a relic of her mother to cry over, over and over again. And...

Bentley the Stuffed Crow himself! What I wouldn't pay to see Eliza's face when she opens up that little *Wunderkammer*.

Speaking of sentimental knickknacks, after the Lambert-Keaton trials, they let me keep one of the red coolers. I never travel without it. In another time, it would have been perfect for smuggling hash across international borders. But now I use it mainly for cigarettes. I don't smoke much. Maybe a drag or two every few weeks. Eliza would have my head if she ever found out. That's what killed her mother, after all.

But in Paris especially, the smell of unfiltered Pall Malls brings back memories.

I don't know if this is the same cooler I took to North Korea—the *famous* cooler. They tell me it is. There were at least four or five dozen coolers just like it designed and manufactured somewhere in the subterranean laboratories of InfraGen Tech. I never knew where exactly.

I did, however, get to see the insides of the SHEM Project. Twice. The first time was with Dustin, the kid, on his motorbike, when I met Rowan Krasimir and he explained my assignment in North Korea. The second time I drove myself. Admittedly, I got turned around a couple of times on the way up. Every wind turbine was the same as the last, and with no other buildings or structures to guide me, the roads in every direction blurred together like some sort of halluci-nation out of *Alice in Wonderland.*

Finally, after a few detours that landed me at the foot of a private farm or the entrance to a cattle ranch or another dead end, I rounded a nondescript corner and saw the fifteen-foot barbwire fence and the little industrial guardhouse that I remembered from my previous visit.

The guard was a different fellow than before. He stepped out of the guardhouse with his hand on the holster of a Glock 22. He eyed my BMW suspiciously. I'd been driving the same car for almost six years, but I'd kept it in mint condition. One thing my dad had taught me was how to take good care of a car.

He stepped up to the driver's-side door. I rolled down the window.

"Jim Frost," I said, and I flashed my driver's license. "I should be in the system."

The guard nodded like he already knew all about it, or he didn't care one way or the other. He leaned forward and peered into the rear compartment. The red cooler was sitting perfectly centered on the backseat.

The guard registered no look of recognition or confusion or alarm. Nothing.

"Could you pop your trunk, please?" he said gruffly as he stepped around the car.

I complied. After all, he had a gun, and I didn't.

"One moment," he said, slamming the trunk shut.

Then he reentered the guardhouse and returned with a yellow pass.

"No visitors after six o'clock," he said. "Make sure you sign out as you leave." And he opened the gate.

I parked at the top of the hill in a spot that was labeled, "Visitor Parking Only." I was jet-lagged and tired from my all-inclusive stay in the Democratic People's Republic of

Korea. And I smelled like crap seeing as I'd come straight from the airport.

I had been gone almost a week, but it felt like an eternity. North Korea was no place I'd ever choose for a getaway. And although it was, in essence, a *vacation*, with sightseeing and gourmet dinners and luxury hotels, the experience of having someone looking over your shoulder every time you needed to take a piss wasn't exactly my idea of a holiday.

The whole time I'd posed as Alex Whittier from Twin Falls, Idaho. I played the part of a young, single graduate student traveling abroad for the summer. To keep it simple, I said I was getting a master's in physical education. Easy enough. The other two Americans were single men, too, both in their late thirties or early forties and best friends since birth. They called themselves "international thrill seekers." They had just finished climbing Everest. They said North Korea was a pit stop on the way to Alaska, where they were going to try their hands at king crab fishing.

They reminded me a lot of my dad's best friend, Rick Milliken, the notorious treasure hunter.

The tour group was made up of only twelve people. The nine others were from Canada and Australia. I didn't get to know any of them very well. I kept to myself and said as little as possible so as to remain inconspicuous. I was, after all, *incognito*.

The Koryo travel agency had confiscated our passports when we landed in Pyongyang, and we didn't see them again until we were boarding the plane to leave. The whole time I invented scenarios in which the North Korean government discovered my passport was a fake and carted me off to prison camp, where I'd spend the rest of my days scratching tallies in a granite wall and whittling blunt daggers out of bars of soap.

But as it was, the experience proved to be entirely painless, except for the nervous moment in the metro station when I made contact with Rowan's inside man. Otherwise, the tour was nothing more than an international field trip with a couple of very fussy chaperones.

And the result? There it sat, centered perfectly, in the backseat of my 2007 BMW. The contents of the red cooler.

There were a few other cars parked in the lot, each of them in designated spots with initials. There was a beat-up 1984 Honda Civic parked in the spot labeled "R. K."— Rowan Krasimir. For a car that was almost thirty years old, I'd say it was in pretty good shape. But I also had to wonder how this guy could afford to pay me fifty grand for what amounted to an all-expenses-paid vacation in East Asia and not afford a nicer ride for himself.

The automatic doors at the main entrance of the building slid open as I approached. Just inside, a young receptionist greeted me and asked me to take a seat. She picked up the phone and exchanged a few words with somebody on the other end, and then she stood and said, "Follow me."

I clutched the red cooler instinctively. It hadn't left my side since North Korea.

The receptionist swiped her badge and led me through a nondescript white door into a long, sterile hallway.

On my first visit, the receptionist had taken me through a door marked "Administration," down a flight of stairs, across a hall, and into a small subterranean office. I had found Rowan Krasimir at a desk peering down his long nose at a jumble of code on a computer screen.

He had said, without looking up from the monitor, "Greta tells me you're my man."

But this time the receptionist coasted past the door marked "Administration" and led me to another door, farther down. It was labeled "SHEM Labs." Here she swiped her badge again and instructed me to enter. The first room was a small antechamber with a sink and an emergency eye-rinsing device. There were stacks of freshly pressed lab coats in a large cupboard, and safety goggles and latex gloves.

"Suit up," she said.

When I had pulled on a lab coat and goggles and gloves, the receptionist punched a code into the keypad on the wall and ushered me through another door.

We entered a wide, low chamber cluttered with technicians in white coats bent over trays and microscopes and vials of yellow fluid. Not a single one looked up when we came in.

I waited in the doorway while the receptionist signaled to one of the technicians.

It was Rowan Krasimir.

"Jim Frost," he said walking over. He clasped my hand warmly. "Thank you," he said to the receptionist.

She smiled and slipped out the door.

"So you made it back in one piece," he said.

"Yes, sir."

"Good, good," he said, his eyes darting from me to something on a nearby monitor. "One moment, if you don't mind." He turned and gave some instructions to a huddle of technicians. Then he turned back to face me squarely. "So are you ready for the grand tour?"

"Sure," I said. "If you have time. But I have no idea what any of this is."

"You are standing in the heart of the Seed Hibernation

and Environmental Management facility," he said. "This is the primary lab were geneticists map and catalogue DNA codes."

"Dustin said something about genetics," I said, trying to put two and two together.

"Yes," said Rowan. "All my technicians are trained biogeneticists. That's how I found Greta. Her former advisor is a colleague of mine."

He was talking about Gerard Boule.

Rowan led me across the room to a set of glass doors.

He continued, "She's quite a find, Greta."

"Uh-hum," I murmured, unsure of his meaning.

"It's too bad I had to ground her," he said, "She is our best agent. She has an instinct for this kind of work. She can spot an RGV a mile away. She usually has some basic sequencing equipment in the field, but you try running an SEQ when you're being chased by the KPA."

"Uh-huh," I said.

We passed through the glass doors into a narrow room with several large machines lining the walls.

"The Dehydration Lab," Rowan explained, walking straight through to a door on the other side. "This is where we prepare the seeds for storage."

We passed into another room, almost identical to the first.

There was a buzz coming from somewhere, I think a large ventilator on the opposite wall.

"She must like you quite a bit," Rowan said over the din, "or she wouldn't have recommended you."

He took me out into a hallway where there was an elevator. He pushed the call button.

We took the lift up two floors and emerged in the blinding light of day. We had, in fact, emerged in a steamy antechamber that marked the entrance to a large greenhouse. The midafternoon sunlight streamed through the glass panels in the ceiling.

"This is where we work on our tans." Rowan chuckled.

He punched a code into a control box and ushered me into the greenhouse. Rows of shallow planters were arranged like squares on a checkerboard across long tables. In each planter, there were sprouts in various stages of growth, some just seedlings, others tall and budding.

"The Regeneration Room," Rowan said. "Just one of our six greenhouses."

He examined a few of the saplings carefully. There was a woman on the far side of the room. He called her over, and they exchanged some words in what sounded like Russian. Then he turned back to me.

"Seeds have expiration dates, too, you know," he said.

"Sometimes we have to harvest new seeds from old ones before our stores expire." He indicated the little trays of recently harvested seeds. "Although under the right conditions, many seeds can remain viable for hundreds or even thousands of years."

"What constitutes the right conditions?" I asked.

"I'm glad you asked." He grinned.

We took the elevator down twenty stories. Rowan explained that the facility had been built deep into limestone bedrock, where the temperature was naturally cooler. The building was retrofitted and reinforced and protected against every natural disaster imaginable.

"It's even bombproof," he said on the ride down, "at least where we're headed now. Safest place you could find yourself during a nuclear attack."

"Are you expecting a nuclear attack anytime soon?" I asked.

Rowan smiled as if I had said something amusing.

When the elevator doors slid open, a gust of ice-cold air rushed into the cabin. Artificial light from a thousand fluorescent bulbs streamed in. The chamber we stepped into was the size of an airplane hangar and lined floor to ceiling with glowing glass tubes. The floor of the chamber was littered with what appeared to be hundreds of bookshelves, all crammed together like stacks of dominoes. Here, too, the shelves were divided into compartments, each containing a glowing glass tube. Scattered about the room were little electric carts with mechanical ladders that extended into the ozone.

"Welcome to the Vault." Rowan grinned.

My fingers were numb from the cold. I shivered.

"We keep it at two below zero at all times," Rowan explained, "but we also have a few smaller vaults for seeds that fare better in more moderate climates."

"There must be thousands," I said.

"Millions," Rowan said, grinning with childlike excitement. "Come look at this."

He led me across the floor and down one of the many aisles that wove between the towering shelves. We came to row 16A, and Rowan turned the crank. The shelves groaned on their tracks, and, like Moses parting the Red Sea, an aisle appeared between 16A and 16B.

Rowan led me down the narrow pass, his eyes searching the expanses of glowing tubes, which I now saw were canisters, each carefully insulated with several layers of translucent fiberglass.

Rowan stopped in front of a canister labeled "PA-xiv."

He released a valve on the underside of the canister, and it let out a hiss as it detached from the wall.

Rowan held the canister out for me to see. The seeds were visible through a clear plastic window in the frosted fiberglass—maybe a dozen or so black specks sitting like royalty on a little white cushion.

"*Papaver metus rhodai*," he said, "a variety of poppy believed to be extinct until only recently. This is one of yours."

He replaced the canister and then led me to the other end of the vault. This time he had to climb a ladder some fifteen feet to find what he was looking for.

When he returned to ground level, he had another canister. This one looked a little more primitive than the first. Through the viewing window I could see a handful of yellow flecks on a foam sponge.

"*Solanum lycopersicum nihil*," he said, "a type of heirloom tomato grown in the Northern Himalayas. This was your very first delivery."

"How do you know that?" I asked.

"It's all catalogued in our system. The agent who identifies the RGV, the sandwich guy who delivers it, meaning you in this case, the date of delivery, et cetera. I checked the database before you arrived."

He showed me ink scribbles on the palm of his hand indicating which canisters were mine.

"I see." My head was buzzing. It felt like I had walked onto the set of *2001: A Space Odyssey*. The humming ventilation system. The translucent tubes that made the place look like an alien spacecraft.

And all for what? *Seeds?*

"Okay, so let's see what you've got for me this time," Rowan said eagerly.

I had forgotten I was carrying the cooler. I handed it over without protest. After all, he was paying me fifty grand for it.

Rowan turned the cooler upside down, like he had shown me on my first visit to his office, and then, with both thumbs, he pressed the round dimples in the base of the chest, smooth indentations that were almost invisible to the untrained eye. The cooler gave a sigh, and a sixteen-square-inch compartment fell out of the belly of the cooler.

Neatly folded into this compartment was a clear plastic baggie. Rowan held the baggie up to the light.

There they were. Eight golden kernels.

Zea mays matris, I explained to the court.
Zea mays matris. In other words, corn.

279

There used to be hundreds of varieties. This particular type was harvested exclusively in the mountain villages of Pyongan-namdo.

Well, certainly, yes.

Rowan Krasimir did.

I had nothing to do with that.

No, I was never invited back.

Again, that was all Mr. Krasimir.

I'm not a geneticist, so I really can't say.

No, I couldn't tell you that either.

Well, that's easy. Because Zea mays matris is the only variety of corn on the planet known to be immune to Fetter's Rot.

CHAPTER 32

THE MAIL FINALLY came today. It has been delayed two weeks because the manager of the building took a holiday and forgot to have the post forwarded to our pied-à-terre. All our mail has been piling up on the floor of his downstairs office these past couple weeks, unbeknownst to us, and finally today we got a stack several inches thick from a very apologetic young woman whom I believe to be the building manager's eldest daughter.

If I were a younger man or she were an older woman, we might get along very well, the building manager's eldest daughter and I.

There were several items in there for Spencer, stuff having to do with his job back home. There were also several letters from Eugene's paranoid agent in New York.

Apparently he received the *Jolly Roger* manuscript and *loved it!* He just had a few notes on the character of the badly burned space captain. He wanted to know more about the nuclear blast that melted off the captain's face. How it came to be. What had happened to Earth. Et cetera.

Eugene's going to try to fit it in somewhere that the nuclear blast went off in New Delhi in 2198, when the captain was but a wee lad combing a deserted shipyard with his father. Turns out the captain's father was a junk dealer specializing in used spaceships—my idea, inspired by my very own junk dealer father.

When the bomb goes off right there in New Delhi Square, marking the beginning of the end of Earth, the captain's father is blown to a billion tiny bits. *Everyone* within a fifty-mile radius is blown to a billion tiny bits. But by some miracle of miracles, the captain, a small boy then, is spared. He happens to be digging around in the torn-up cockpit of an old Indian Starfighter. The radon-enforced blast shield of the Starfighter protects the boy from the worst of the nuclear explosion, and the boy emerges badly burned but alive in a completely barren wasteland.

That was my idea, too.

Apparently, several Russian military rescue crews arrive on the scene and find the young boy, the lone survivor of the blast, and take him aboard a Russian Galaxy Fighter and fit him with robotic tissue replacements and all that. Somehow, in all the confusion of all-out nuclear war and the destruction of Earth, the Galaxy Fighter loses contact with the Russian space fleet, and the boy finds himself the adopted member of a renegade space crew.

What do you think?

We think it'll sell.

Eugene's got some work ahead of him now, fitting all *that* into the story. And he already has *his* eighty thousand words.

Not me. Not me. Sorry, Sam.

There were a couple of things in the mail for me, too. One was a letter from Duncan. He must have sent it just before he died. Magnum Opus. He's got a picture in there of him and Greta standing on the Pont des Arts with the river Seine flowing under them, and the sun setting over the Louvre. The railings of the Pont des Arts are littered with silver and gold padlocks, which couples fasten to the bridge as tokens of their love, and which are glittering in the pinkish light of the setting sun.

Greta and Duncan are both very young in the photograph. Duncan has a full head of hair, and Greta looks like she could still be in high school. I flipped the picture over. On the back, scrawled in Greta's familiar handwriting, it reads, "Paris 2004."

Duncan writes, "I thought you'd get a kick out of this photograph. Hard to recognize us from way back when. Who are those people? Ghosts."

The second item that came for me is from Pilar Rochac. She has written a note saying that the house on Gough Street is in good shape and not to hurry home because it is terribly hot and humid in the city. Several elderly people have died in their homes from heatstroke, she says, and the city has just issued an air quality alert.

"It's not the San Francisco I grew up in," she writes. She immigrated to San Francisco with her mother in 2014.

Different times. Different times.

Pilar has enclosed a letter from the Vatican, which came for me in late July and which she felt ought to be forwarded to me immediately since it looked important.

It is an invitation to a ceremonial mass in honor of my sister, the beloved Saint Marilee Lorenzo of San Francisco, as she is being conferred the title of Patron Saint of Earthquakes and Lou Gehrig's Disease.

Magnum Opus.

The final letter comes to me from the FedEx headquarters in Memphis, Tennessee. The chairman and president, Abel

Eisentraut, writes that he is very sorry, but the package I mailed "express" on July 27, 2056, from Paris, France, to San Francisco, New Shasta, United States of America, has been lost in transit. Unfortunately, there is nothing he or his staff can do at this time to recoup the loss. A FedEx representative will notify me immediately if anything turns up.

If.

He ends the letter by thanking me for my business and asking that I continue to choose FedEx for all my future delivery needs.

Eliza has, of course, been on the phone with FedEx all morning. It turns out that if you type the tracking number into an online system, the last place the microchip with my brain, and Greta's urn, and Bentley the Stuffed Crow turn up before vanishing into thin air is the Queen Beatrix International Airport in Aruba.

Do I think Greta is up there somewhere laughing her ass off?

Okay, why not.

ACKNOWLEDGMENTS

THANK YOU to Mom and Dad, the earliest supporters of my work, to Joey, the most judicious, and to Danny, the most enthusiastic. Thank you to Kim Krizan and Dean Gualco for spending time with my work, and for helping me navigate the world of self-publishing. Thank you to Erin, my editor, who only goes by Erin. I also owe a huge thank-you to Tyler Thompson, who appreciated my work when I couldn't stand to look at it, and to Sarah Prestwood, who was Sarah Smock when this book was first conceived. And finally, to the Monkey, who makes this whole monkey parade worthwhile.

ABOUT THE AUTHOR

NICHOLAS PONTICELLO is a high school mathematics teacher in Los Angeles, where he lives with the art historian Nico Machida and their five freshwater fish. Nicholas received degrees in mathematics and astrophysics from the University of California, Berkeley in 2006. He is the creator of the web-comic *Simply Nick*. *Do Not Resuscitate* is his first novel.

For more titles by this author, please visit www.booleanop.com.

Made in the USA
San Bernardino, CA
05 October 2016